FACE DOWN IN THE GRAVE

Thomas O

VELOX BOOKS
Published by arrangement with the author.

Face Down in the Grave copyright © 2023
by Thomas O.

All Rights Reserved.

This book is a work of fiction. People, places, events, and situations are the product of the author's imagination. Any resemblance to actual persons, living or dead, or historical events, is purely coincidental.

No part of this book may be reproduced, stored in a retrieval system, or transmitted by any means without the written permission of the author and publisher.

CONTENTS

And the Universe Blinked _____ 1

Face Down in the Grave _____ 27

Taffy Bomb _____ 39

Decamonoprogeny _____ 51

The Well, the Wheel, and Wilhelm _____ 69

Ghost Falconry! _____ 81

A Delicious Revenge _____ 113

AND THE UNIVERSE BLINKED

It was nearly five a.m., and my son Fredrick still wasn't back from the dead. "It will happen early," Gabriella had promised me. "You'll be able to spend most of the day with him."

I was shaky—nervous. *What if he doesn't remember me? What if something goes wrong?* But what could go wrong? I'd done my part—paid for this day in blood, and I had been assured that everything would work out smoothly.

Even though he had passed away when he was five, he would be coming back to me from a time when he was a three-year-old. What did he like to do at that age? The park, the zoo, the merry-go-round? Actually, all of those if I remembered correctly.

I stayed in my bedroom as instructed. "Listen for him," I'd been told. "You'll hear him waking up in his bed. He'll call to you." His bedroom, which had been stripped bare in the years after his death, had been hurriedly slapped back together as best as I could remember. His toddler bed was pulled from the garage rafters, his nightstand and lamp reclaimed from a dusty corner of the attic, and some toys were retrieved from the moth-eaten boxes in the hall closet.

As the first morning rays of sunlight poked their way through the crack between the curtains, I heard a small body tossing and turning in the other room. I held my breath.

"Daddy? Mommy?"

I bolted from my bed, almost tripping over my own feet in my haste to get to his bedroom. And there he was—real. His yawn turned into a smile as he saw me enter the room. Without hesitating, I grabbed him in a big bear hug.

"Good morning, Daddy." His voice sounded so young, so cute. Fredrick was exactly as I remembered him. His voice wavered a bit as he glanced around the room. "Hey where's Bossy at?"

Bossy? I paused in thought for a second. "Ohhh, Bossy Bear... he's in the wash. He got dirty last night." It was a lie, of course. Bossy was long gone. Fredrick contemplated this development and then nodded his head as if to say okay. He looked around the rest of his room. Things were not as they were supposed to be—I had done my best, but of course the room wouldn't be exactly as Fredrick was used to. Thankfully, he didn't seem overly concerned by it.

Not wanting to waste a single moment of the day, I picked him up and held him close. "We're going to go to the zoo today," I said. "And then we'll go to the park. We're going to have a lot of fun, just you and me."

"What about Mommy?"

"She's at work. She has to be there all day." This was the second lie in less than a minute. I didn't even know where my ex-wife was living, much less what her work schedule was.

I made him his favorite breakfast: scrambled eggs with some cheese on top. He gobbled them up. Since it was still early, we cuddled up on the couch after breakfast, where I read some of his favorite books to him.

Later that morning, we drove to the zoo. We roared at the lions, beat our chests at the monkeys, and made faces at the bears. We fed the goats and rode the merry-go-round... as many times as he wanted. Fredrick loved every second of it. I took him home for lunch and a nap. I almost hated to let him fall asleep, knowing this was the only day I'd have with him, but I remembered how cranky he'd get, so I let him doze on the couch for a bit. In the afternoon, we went to the park. Not our local park, mind you, but the big one that had the giant dinosaur-shaped climbing structures. We ascended them together; they must've seemed like mountains to him. He laughed in glee as we got to the top.

For dinner we had meatballs and spaghetti, his favorite meal. Ice cream was for dessert, and there was no reason not to let him have a second bowl. He had his bath and then we plopped onto his bed where I read books to him.

He started yawning. Our day was drawing to a close. I blinked my eyes to fight back the tears.

"Fredrick?" I said. He looked up at me. "I want you to always remember that I love you. No matter where you're at, I love you."

"Okay," he said. "I love you too." I stroked his hair as he yawned again. His eyelids fluttered a few times and then slowly came together. After he fell asleep, I continued to hold him. Soon, I fell asleep too. I woke up a little after midnight. I was alone, and the house was cold and cavernous. I fetched my phone from my pocket and sent a text to Gabriella. *I want one more.*

***

I'd made one little mistake that I didn't even realize at the time—my neighbor Emmett had seen us leaving the house on our way to the zoo. The next day I ran into him as I dragged my trashcan out to the curb. "Good morning!" he said along with a wave of his hand.

I looked up reluctantly. "Hey Emmett," I said. At one point, he and I had been close friends, but after Fredrick died, and I began isolating myself, we'd drifted apart.

"How's everything going?" he said. "It seems like we haven't talked for ages."

"Everything's fine," I replied, trying my best to sound polite yet uninterested at the same time.

"I saw you had a child over yesterday…"

I froze, immediately understanding the direction this conversation was about to head. I decided to answer the question he was thinking before he even asked it. "It was my sister's kid. Looks a lot like Freddy did, no?"

"Yeah, that's kinda what I was thinking." This was followed by an awkward silence while I looked Emmett right in the eyes. This was a man who, at one point several years earlier, I could've confided in. Heck, he was Fredrick's godfather.

"Emmett, I just lied to you right now. That wasn't my nephew, that was Fredrick himself."

I could see Emmett's confusion etch itself in the lines of his brow. "What do you mean?"

"How many meaningless days do you think you've lived through? I'm talking about days that you don't even remember—days that have no impact whatsoever on what happens to you for the rest of your life."

"I'm not really sure. A whole lot, I guess," he replied.

"Well, just imagine if someone could be pulled out from one of those past meaningless days and brought into the present, and you could spend the day with them. Wouldn't that be great? I asked.

Emmett nodded his head.

"And then," I continued, "they would be sent back, but it wouldn't affect anything in the past because it was a meaningless day to begin with."

"I'm not sure what you're getting at…"

I decided to let him off the hook with a chuckle. "Sorry, Emmett, that was just a bad joke. He was my nephew. Nothing more to it than that." My phone buzzed in my pocket—it had certainly taken her long enough to respond. "See you around, Emmett," I said as I turned and headed back into my house.

I fished in my pocket and checked the text message from Gabriella. *Same cost.*

I'd have to kill again. I was hoping the second time would be easier.

***

Gabriella owned and ran a small restaurant. She was half my age, but twice as smart and probably four times as dangerous. I went to see her before the evening service so that the restaurant would be empty. I entered shortly after three p.m. and took a booth. She saw me and sat down across from me. "The day went well, it seems," she said with a hint of arrogance.

"Yeah, as good as I'd hoped for."

Gabriella glanced over at the entrance to make sure nobody else was about to enter the restaurant, and then reached through the neckline of her shirt and pulled out a ruby amulet, which was held around her neck by a thin chain. She grasped it tight in her right hand while offering me her other hand. "Let's find a meaningless day," she said.

I reached out and grabbed her left hand as her eyes closed. Within a moment, a faint glow emanated from the gaps between the fingers of her right hand. Only the sound of our breathing filled the restaurant as I waited for her to find a day. Eventually she started talking. "I can see a day... he's almost three years old. You were at work. Your wife stayed with him. He played with his car collection and showed you his favorite truck when you returned home, but you didn't really look at it. You had spaghetti for dinner. Do you remember?"

"Of course I don't."

"Okay, that's where we'll pull him from. And now for your payment." She reached down into her apron pocket and pulled out a photograph. "The name and address are on the back," she said as she slid it across the table to me.

I glanced at the photo. A man—middle-aged and unremarkable. I couldn't imagine why anyone would want him dead, but it didn't really matter. Gabriella apparently had a hit list she was working off of, and this guy was next. I didn't know where this list had come from, but I figured anyone whose name was on it had done something to deserve it. I put the photo in my shirt pocket and looked back at Gabriella. "Will he remember our days together? After he goes back, will he have any idea that he's been sent into the future?"

"He won't have any specific memories—he can't. Nothing that happens now can affect the past, but it all will become part of the fabric of who he is... or was. That's how my father explained it to me anyway."

I patted my shirt pocket. "I have a job to do. I'll let you know when it's done."

***

Adan Halford was the name of my next victim. He lived about ten miles away. The next night, I drove over there and parked a block away from his house, walking the rest of the way. When I got to the home it was completely unlit, as if nobody was home. A quick visual scan of the area showed no sign of surveillance cameras. I hadn't necessarily intended on doing the deed right then. Mostly I was just checking the place out, but it looked like I might have a good opportunity. There were no streetlights, and the houses were spaced far apart. I could see no meaningful security measures in place at all. Adan Halford was not expecting this. I hid along the side of the house, figuring that I'd give him an hour. If he came back within that time, and he was alone, he would die.

Twenty minutes later my plan bore fruit. Two minivan headlights came from down the street and turned into the driveway. From my position on the side of the house, I could see that my mark was the driver. Aside from him, the vehicle was empty.

Adan's car crept slowly up the driveway. A few moments later, he killed the engine and got out of the car. At the same time, I stepped out purposefully from the side of the house. He gasped at the sight of me pulling a length of cord from my back pocket as I sprang toward him. This guy… he looked like an average boring suburbanite, not the kind of dirtbag I was hoping for. But still, he was on Gabriella's hit list. He must've done something to deserve this. Giving him no chance to scream, I raised my hands and lunged at him. The cord fit around his neck perfectly, like it belonged there the whole time. His eyes widened as my muscles tensed up and drew the cord taut around his throat. He put up a bit of a struggle—scratching and clawing, but I outweighed him by at least a hundred pounds, and he didn't last too long before he fell to the ground lifeless. I surveyed the area one final time to see if I was still in the clear. It was at this point that I noticed a child's car seat strapped into the car. I stepped closer and saw a peacefully sleeping little girl belted snuggly into the seat. My god, how could I have missed that? I had the brief thought that maybe I should take the child out of her seat and put her someplace safe, but then I realized that she was already in as safe a place as I could realistically leave her. Someone would come along eventually and discover both her and her dead father. She would be okay. It was time for me to leave, and so I stepped away from the scene and blended back into the night. When I got home, I burned the photo of Adan Halford in my fireplace, and then I threw up.

***

"You told me all these people on your lists were dirtbags! You know, the kind of people who deserved what they had coming to them!" I yelled as Gabriella emerged from the back of the restaurant.

She looked around furiously as she approached my booth. The restaurant was empty, but that didn't stop her from shushing me. "Keep it down," she implored. She sat next to me. "I assure you they all deserve to have you come knocking at their door."

"Yeah, but this guy seemed like some random suburban dad."

Gabriella looked disappointed with me. "Appearances can be deceiving. Just because someone doesn't look harmless doesn't mean they can't rip your face off. Figuratively speaking, of course," she said.

I wasn't even listening to her excuses. "Just give me what you owe me and then we're done."

Gabriella's tone softened. "I'm sorry. I guess this time was a lot harder than the first. Maybe I should've given you a different target."

"My God, what have I done?" I asked.

"You've earned yourself another day with your dead son, that's what you've done. You've earned a chance to hear him laugh, a chance to tell him you love him one last time. That's what you should be focusing on."

"I'm going to make it count. I won't be back here."

She smiled knowingly. "Get a good night's rest if you can. He'll be there when you wake up in the morning."

I went home. Everything from his last visit was still set up. He'd be a bit younger this time, but not by much. I planned out a great day. There was a little amusement park not too far away that was geared toward small children—the perfect place to go. It would make for an unforgettable final day.

***

The first part of the morning went as planned. I woke up and hurried to his bedroom and hugged him as if it had been years since I'd seen him last, though it'd only been a few days. We ate breakfast and had a little playtime at home. Once we were ready to leave, we walked out to the car, and I placed Fredrick in his car seat. As I pulled his belt tight, I heard Emmett's voice behind me. "Good morning!"

Shit. "Good morning, Emmett!" I said as I stood upright, positioning myself to block Fredrick from his view.

Emmett walked over from his yard without seeming to notice Fredrick. "Wow! I actually get to talk to you two times in the same week. I'm glad you're finally starting to get out of your house."

"Yeah, I guess I've been shutting myself away for too long now."

"Hey, you should come over for dinner tonight," he offered with a sudden burst of energy. "We're going to be barbequing. We'd love to see you again. It'll be like old times."

"Thank you, but tonight's not good."

Emmett's voice turned serious. "It's been too long. We miss you. You've got to start living again."

I opened my mouth to speak when Fredrick beat me to it. "Hi Emmett!" he said with a wave.

Emmett peered around me into the vehicle. His face scrunched up as he saw the child in my car. "Hey there, little guy. You're the one I saw the other day."

Fredrick smiled in return. "We're going to ride the train!" he said.

Emmett started to respond. "Well, it sounds like you're going to have a good ti…" But he couldn't finish his sentence. Instead, he gasped and started grabbing at his chest. "I don't feel so well," he puffed.

I grabbed his elbow to steady him. "Can you walk? Let's get you a seat," I said as I guided him up his driveway and over to a bench on his porch, all the while yelling out for his wife Mona. As soon as he sat down, he seemed to feel a little better.

His breathing returned to normal, and the color came back to his face.

Mona came out of the house after hearing the commotion. "Emmett, are you okay?" she asked in a panic.

"I think so," he said. "I'm not sure what happened."

"I should call 911," Mona said, unconvinced.

"No," he insisted. "I think I'm okay."

I stayed with Emmett for a few minutes. Thankfully, his recovery from the malaise was as quick as its onset. Once I was sure he was doing okay, I turned to Mona. "It looks like he's doing better. But keep an eye on him for now."

Mona agreed, and I excused myself as politely as I could. I'd already wasted too many precious minutes and I just wanted to get the heck out of there. "Take care, both of you," I said as I backed away.

Emmett glanced over to my car, where Fredrick was still strapped into his seat, and oddly enough, he shuddered, as if a cold wind had just chilled him. "What's... what's going on?" he asked.

I didn't answer. I was already halfway down the driveway anyway. I gave them a wave and returned to my car. A small part of me felt like a horrible friend, abandoning Emmett when he probably could've used me the most, but each second of this day was valuable, and I'd paid far too much to have any of them wasted.

Fredrick and I resumed our day, and we both had a blast. Every laugh and giggle that emanated from him was pressed into my mind where I kept it safe. We ended the night at home, with me reading him all his favorite stories. "Would you like another?" I kept asking him. He happily accepted each time, until he finally got drowsy, giving big yawns as I worked my way through the last few pages. This was it, my last chance to tell him how much I loved him. "Fredrick, I want you to always remember that..." The sudden sound of shattering glass broke my train of thought. Someone was breaking in through a window.

I shot up and ran down the stairs, only to see Emmett standing in the entryway. His hands, arms and legs were all bloodied and cut from smashing through the window and climbing inside. "Emmett, what the hell's going on?" I demanded.

"It's not right. Something's not right," he stammered. He was shaking uncontrollably. "Things aren't okay," he muttered.

"No, everything's okay," I assured him as I guided him to the couch and had him sit down. "Stay here, let me get Mona over here."

I ran next door and got Mona, who followed me back to my house. We tended to his wounds. Fortunately, none of the cuts were deep enough to cause serious bleeding. However, his mental status didn't seem to get any better. He just kept mumbling that everything was "off" and "wrong." Finally, Mona talked him into following her back home, assuring me that she would have him checked out at the emergency room. As soon as they were gone, my concern for Emmett faded as I ran up the stairs, desperately hoping to get in my last moments with Fredrick before he either fell asleep, or worse, simply disappeared. When I made it to his doorway, I saw that his bed was empty. He was gone, and the house was freezing cold. I felt lonelier than ever.

God damn Emmett—he'd ruined my last moments with Fredrick. I couldn't let it end that way. I pulled my phone from my pocket and called Gabriella. She answered without even bothering to say hello. "I thought I might hear from you again," she said.

"One more. But make it someone awful, not some random soccer dad."

"You're breaking up," she said. "I can't hear you through the static. Come see me in a couple of days." Then she hung up.

***

Sitting across from me in the booth of her restaurant, Gabriella pushed a photograph toward me. "He's the worst of the bunch. Name and address are on the back."

I glanced down at the photo. The guy didn't look so bad. I mean, there was nothing about his appearance that screamed *horrible person*. "You sure?"

"Yeah. Drunk driver. Killed a mother and child. And that was after his license had already been taken away for earlier drunk driving arrests. The guy served only three years in prison and was completely unrepentant. He had a pretty good lawyer, apparently."

"Maybe I should go after the lawyer," I said drolly.

"Do that on your own time. The lawyer's not on my list," she said sternly.

"What is this list of yours, anyway? Just a bunch of drunk drivers?"

"No, it's not that at all." Gabriella held up the photo. "This man isn't on my list because he's a drunk driver. The fact that he killed anyone at all is unrelated to my needs, but it's helpful if it makes things easier for you. Beyond that, I think the payment you're receiving is substantial enough for you not to ask any more questions."

"Of course," I said. "Now about my payment…"

She retrieved her amulet and held out her hands. "Let's find another meaningless day."

***

I have to admit that after my second murder, my faith in Gabriella had been shaken. Why I even trusted her to begin with, I'm not sure. Maybe I just wanted my son back so badly that I lost myself for a while. This time, I wasn't about to trust her until I did some research of my own. I went to the library to use their computer. I was quickly becoming a mass murderer, so I figured it would be better to use a public computer that couldn't be traced back to me personally. The man's name was Jackson Rose, and he was indeed a total piece of shit. In addition to his drunk driving murders, he had several arrests for spousal abuse and child endangerment. Heck, this was someone I might've even killed for free. I made sure to clear my search history and wipe the keyboard clean before leaving.

When I returned to my house, I saw a bookish, mousy little man standing in my front yard, trying to get a look into one of my living room windows. *Who the hell was this?*

I parked the car and got out slowly, my agitation growing. "Who are you?" I demanded of him.

He fumbled for his words. "Uhh, do you… do you live here?"

I nodded my head. "Yes, and whatever you're selling, or whatever the hell you think you're doing, I don't want any part of it. Leave." I must've outweighed the guy by a hundred and fifty pounds, nonetheless I stood as tall as possible to increase my intimidation factor.

"I'm sorry to bother you," he said, "but this house seems to be the focal point of a huge disruption. I've felt it twice now."

I walked past the man toward my front door. "I wouldn't know anything about that. Get the Hell out of here. Last warning."

"Please," he begged, "I just want to talk to you. Whatever's happening here is extremely dangerous. It's almost as if the universe itself has been knocked off balance."

I had no idea who this guy was, but he clearly wasn't with the police—he was too mousy, too frightened. I paused before stepping into my house. "Really? That's odd, I didn't feel anything." I began to close the door.

The guy lit up at my momentary decision to engage him. "Wait!" he exclaimed as he jammed an arm inside my house to prevent me from closing the door completely. "Most people can't feel the fissures that knock the universe off balance, but I can. And from what I can tell, whatever happened emanated from here. It's like following the cracks in a window back to the point where it got hit by a rock. It took me a few days to find it," his eyes did a sweep of the area to confirm his theory, "but this is the spot."

"Fissures? In the universe?"

He nodded. "Yes, that's the easiest way to explain it without going too into detail."

"Time for you to go. This is your last warning before I call the police."

He looked me up and down, trying to get a read on me. "I don't think you're going to call the police at all. I think you want nothing to do with them," he said, as some sort of inner confidence began to emerge.

"Okay, well maybe I won't waste their time. Maybe I'll just snap your little neck and bury you in my yard." That was probably the more realistic of the two threats, but still a bluff.

The man gulped, but stayed his course. "I just want to talk to you for a few minutes."

"No!" I said as I shoved his arm out of the doorway and slammed the door shut. I stayed in my living room, peering out at the man through my curtains. He stood on my doorstep for a couple of minutes, I guess with the hope that I would reemerge. Finally, he retreated into a sedan parked on the street where he just sat and watched my house. Bastard.

This was a disturbing new development, but I was determined to spend one last day with my son, and nothing was going to stop me. Not the little mousy man. Not some invisible, moronic "fissures" knocking the universe off balance. Nothing.

I'm not sure what time I went to sleep, but at four in the morning I was woken by the sound of two men yelling outside of my house. One of the voices belonged to Emmett. I shot up out of bed and ran downstairs to my living room window where I could get a good look outside. There, I saw mouse-man from the night before standing outside of his car, apparently trying to calm Emmett down.

I flung my front door open and ran outside. "Emmett, Emmett," I called out. "It's okay."

Emmett diverted his attention from mouse-man and turned toward me. "It's not right," he said. "Things aren't okay."

I glared at mouse-man. "What did you do to him?"

"I didn't do anything," he replied. "I fell asleep in my car, then the next thing I knew he was out here pounding on my windows." He took a long look at Emmett. "But I think I know what's wrong with him."

"Wait here!" I said to mouse-man as I began leading Emmett back to his house. "C'mon, Emmett. It'll be okay, you just need to rest."

I gently put my arm around him and walked him to his house. The front door had been left open, so I called out to Mona, who came running in her nightgown when she heard my voice. "Emmett!" she gasped. "What are you doing?"

Whatever fugue he might've been in seemed to recede when he heard Mona's voice. "Mona?" he said weakly. "Help me to bed, please."

Mona put her arm around him and slowly led him back to their bedroom. A minute later, she returned. "What happened?" she asked.

"I could ask you the same thing. I woke up with him yelling in front of my house."

"He seemed okay last night," she said. "I thought he'd recovered from whatever had been affecting him. Other than the cuts on his legs and arms, they didn't find anything wrong with him at the emergency room."

"Well, he seems okay for the moment. Keep an eye on him and I'll check back with you in a bit," I said.

I stormed away from Emmett and Mona's house with determined steps, intent on going back to mouse-man and throttling him until I got some answers. "Get inside," I said as I passed by him and went into my house. He followed me obediently. Once we were both inside, I slammed the door. "Talk! What the hell is happening to him?"

Mouse-man thought for a moment, carefully contemplating his words. "It's like this," he said. "There are certain people, like me, who can see and feel the fabric of the universe, so to speak. Your neighbor... Emmett? Is it? I think he's someone like me, maybe just not as strong."

"First of all, he's not JUST my neighbor," I said as I jabbed him in the chest. "He's one of my best friends. He was my son's godfather, for Christ's sake. He's never mentioned any of this 'fabric of the universe' shit to me."

Mouse-man shook his head. "He doesn't even know what he's capable of. Like I said, his ability isn't as strong as mine. The only reason he's feeling these effects at all is because he's right next door to... whatever's happening. If he lived further away, he would probably be fine. It seems like, for the first time in his life, he's feeling the pull of these events. It's been stretching his mind and warping his reality. His brain doesn't know what to make of it. He's confused, mixed up."

"Will he get better?"

"Yes, I think so. His mind just needs some rest, and some time to sort things out—a couple of weeks, maybe."

I paused to contemplate what mouse-man had been saying. Apparently, whatever was affecting Emmett was my fault. I turned my attention back to mouse-man. "Who exactly are you?" I asked.

"My name's Gantry. I volunteered to come here to see what was happening."

"Volunteered?"

"Yes. There's a whole group of us—nothing official, just a loose collection of people who have the gift for seeing through the veil. There's a bunch of us all over the world, and we all felt that something was wrong, but I happen to live closest, so that's why I came to check it out."

"Well Gantry, you can go tell all your little friends that this will all be over soon enough."

"Please, whatever it is you're doing, stop. There's some very powerful magic at work here, and serious consequences for these sorts of things." Gantry glanced around at the decorations on my wall, taking advantage of his time inside to try and learn a little bit about me, it seemed. He walked over to a plaque on the wall, wiped the dust off, and started reading the inscription. "For courage and bravery above and beyond the call of duty, given on this day by the Los Angeles County Fire Department and the Los Angeles County Board of Supervisors." He looked back at me. "Wow. You're a hero. Don't sully it."

He had caught me off guard. "That was a long time ago. I was different back then. I had a family, a job, and... I don't think you need to know anything more about me. You can get out now."

Gantry took one last look at the pictures on my wall—pictures of Fredrick mostly, and then left.

***

Whatever wackadoo bullshit Gantry was peddling didn't concern me, except for the part about Emmett. I planned to go through with my final killing and spend one last day with my boy and give him a proper goodbye, but I had to make sure that Emmett was nowhere nearby when that happened. I spoke with Mona the next day and convinced her to take Emmett on a weekend getaway. "He needs to relax," I explained to her. "Take him down the coast and get some sun." Mona, who was worried and desperate, agreed.

The next thing I had to do was to come up with a plan for killing Jackson Rose, the despicable piece of dirt standing between me and my final day with my son. I spent a day silently following him. My conclusion was that it would be best to kill him in his driveway, just like I'd done with Adan Halford.

The whole time I kept a cautious eye out for Gantry. He was an insignificant speck of a man, but I didn't want to underestimate him. Lucky for him he didn't pop up on my radar, so I continued with my plan. I arrived at Jackson Rose's home just after sunset. I parked a few streets away and walked to his house. I'd made sure to leave my cell phone at home so that its location couldn't be traced. All my tracks were covered, and if everything worked out, I could never be placed at the scene of the murder.

I waited patiently in a dark corner, and within an hour I heard the raucous sound of a way-too-loud car stereo working its way down the street. This guy, most likely driving on a suspended license, seemed to have no discretion whatsoever. He parked his car along the curb in front of his house and slammed his door.

As he walked past, I stepped slowly out of the shadows, emerging behind him unnoticed. Carefully, I pulled a piece of cord from my pocket and stalked up behind him. As he stepped up to his porch, I reached up over him with both arms and pulled the cord back against his throat. His hands shot up to try and pull the cord free, but I summoned as much strength out of my arms as possible, and I could hear his larynx cracking under the pressure. His next move was to reach back with his hands and try to gouge my eyes and scratch my face. He found a little more success this time, landing a big scratch running from my eye to my chin. This only infuriated me and gave me reason to hate him more. I yanked the cord even tighter as the dumb bastard tried and failed to breathe. I'm not sure how long we stayed in that position—seemingly forever, but it was probably just a couple of minutes. His throat cracked one last time as I lowered his limp body to the ground. *Time to get out of here,* I thought. I receded back into the shadows and returned to my car.

A half hour later, I was outside the restaurant. At this time of night it was full of diners, so I didn't bother to enter. Through the window, I was able to make eye contact with Gabriella as she carried plates filled with steaming tacos and burritos. She barely paused as she gave me a slight nod of acknowledgment. I nodded back and then left. I felt good about myself, right up to the point when I saw that fool Gantry standing on the sidewalk right next to where my car was parked, staring right at me.

I stepped up to him and wrenched him toward me by his shirt. "You little prick! Did you follow me?"

Gantry's voice wavered. "I didn't follow you. It was more of an educated guess where you'd be."

I pulled him closer, with my anger clouding my judgment as people on the sidewalk stopped to stare. "A guess?" I said. "That's a pretty good guess. How did you know?" I glanced around at the gawkers. "Get in the car," I commanded him.

Once we were in the car, Gantry nervously opened up. "We were able to hack your phone and check the places you've visited. This is the only place you've been to more than once, aside from your home. I figured you'd show up here again eventually."

My first reaction was an overwhelming wave of anger—anger at the fact that Gantry and his little cronies would have the balls to hack into my phone. But an instant later that was tempered by a sense of relief, since I'd been careful enough to leave my phone at home every time I murdered someone. I thought I would be protecting myself from the police, but it turned out it also may have protected me from this group that Gantry ran with—they most likely didn't know how far I'd gone. "Just who is this loose collection of people you're part of?" I asked.

"Like I said, we're just a group of like-minded individuals, nothing official. But some of us are pretty smart. Once we had your name and address, finding out all about you wasn't too difficult."

"Yeah, well, you don't know everything."

"We will soon enough."

I calculated my odds of killing Gantry and getting away with it—not good. Instead, I began driving to my home in silence, thinking of my next move, with Gantry along for the ride whether he wanted to be or not. Keep your friends close, and your enemies closer. He didn't complain.

After several minutes of awkward silence, Gantry cleared his throat. "It must've been hard coming upon the scene of that accident."

"What accident?" I asked, even though I already knew exactly what he meant. Gantry was poking the bear with a stick. He didn't seem to understand how close I was to reaching over and snapping his little fucking neck.

"Your son and your wife. You were on duty when they crashed. Got the call and went out there with your engine company—didn't know it was them until you pulled up. Your son was already dead."

I gripped the steering wheel until it bent in my hands. Somehow, I kept the car driving straight.

"Your wife survived, but your marriage didn't. She left you a year later."

I turned and screamed. "No! I made her leave. It was her goddamn fault. She ran the red light. She was the one not paying attention. Fredrick died because of her! I got to say goodbye to her, but not to him!"

"I see," Gantry said. "Is that what this is all about? Your wife? Your son?"

Damn it. Gantry had used an emotional crowbar and pried me open like a cheap wooden crate. I could feel my heart slamming against my ribcage as my vision blurred.

He finally seemed to sense that maybe he'd gone a little too far and changed his tack. "That waitress back at the restaurant, I think she possesses the Periculo Manus, the hand of danger. It's that stone she wears around her neck." He looked at me, trying to gauge my reaction, but I was back in control of my emotions. He continued, "There's maybe five objects in the entire world with enough power to unbalance the universe this much. The Periculo Manus is one of them. It's been missing for sixty years until now."

"Never heard of it," I said.

"Most people wouldn't have, unless they're interested in that sort of thing. But now that I've mentioned it, you know what I'm talking about. After all, you've been texting her."

Great, they didn't just have the locations of where my phone had been, but also my texts. There was nothing to be gained by responding to any more of his provocations, so I took a deep breath and simply drove. I had to admit, Gantry and his crew were good at what they did. If they were the police, I'd have been screwed. Maybe I was screwed anyway. It didn't really matter. All I cared about at that moment was my last day with my son, which would be happening shortly. Anything after that was meaningless.

Gantry's gaze fell upon the lines of my face that had grown so much deeper over the previous few years. What they told him, I don't know. He finally broke the silence. "The Periculo Manus was last known to have been in the possession of a man named Tentanum, who was responsible for the deaths of thousands of people."

"Yeah, I don't care."

Gantry ignored me and continued. "You see, the Hand grants many different abilities to its holder, but Tentanum was most interested in the ability to influence people, to bring out the worst in them, and make them do things they might not have otherwise done. He created psychopaths, serial killers—all sorts of homicidal maniacs who spewed death upon the land. Of course, none of the murders could actually be traced back to him, at least not by your typical Johnny Law type, because Tentanum never killed anyone himself. It's a very fascinating story, actually."

He was starting to agitate me again. I glanced down at my hands, which only an hour earlier had been wrapped around the throat of Jackson Rose, the third person I'd killed.

"Anyway," Gantry continued, "to make a very long story short, it became obvious to some people what Tentanum was doing. I mean, if you study the occult, these things jump out at you when you see them. So, a group of people got together and hunted Tentanum down. Not all of them survived, of course, but when they finally got to him, they killed him. And then they tried to burn his body, but it wouldn't burn, so instead they tore it to pieces and buried them all in different parts of the world, just because they were so scared that somehow, he'd return. As for the Hand, it was never recovered. Tentanum didn't have it on him when they finally caught up to him. It just seemed to disappear."

"And this group of people who killed Tentanum, this is the same group you're part of?"

"Oh, so you *do* care," Gantry said, as if he'd scored some points in a non-existent game. "But to answer your question, no. They were mostly just regular people with regular lives. Once he was gone, there was nothing really holding them together as a group. But their story stayed alive, and it's been passed down."

"I only care about your bullshit stories up to the point where they help me figure out who you are. Nothing less, nothing more."

"You want to know who I am? I'm someone who's concerned about what's been going on, especially now that I know the Periculo Manus is involved. Do you know how dangerous that thing is? It feeds on death—the more death that surrounds it, the more powerful it becomes, the more powerful it becomes, the more death it causes. Its power to destroy can become virtually unlimited. Quite a vicious cycle, don't you think?"

I caught the reflection of my face in the rear-view mirror, complete with the bloody scratch running down my cheek. Was that the face of a truly guilty man? All I really wanted was some more time with my son. "Just stop talking," I told Gantry.

A few minutes later, I arrived at my house. I made a nodding motion toward the passenger door, inviting Gantry to get the heck out of my car once it stopped. He got the message and stepped out. "Don't come back," I warned him as I locked the car and walked away. I didn't even glance back to see where that damn twerp wandered off to—there was no point in letting him think I cared. The next day Fredrick would be returned to me. That's all that mattered.

As I tried to fall asleep that night, one thing Gantry spoke of kept me up—that the Periculo Manus had the ability to influence people and bring out the worst in them. I grabbed my phone off my dresser and scrolled through the text messages I'd exchanged with Gabriella. I went to the beginning, back to the time when she was just a stranger who contacted me completely out of the blue. I read that first text again. *Sad? Miserable? I can help.* The weird part is that I'd responded to it—to a text from an unknown person I'd never met before.

No matter. By that point, I was physically tired and emotionally drained. No more thoughts for me that night. I tossed my phone aside and let sleep find me.

***

I had no big plans for the following day—no zoo, no amusement park. Nothing. By this point, I'd learned that it would be safest to stay at home. We would play games and have fun with just each other. Fredrick would return to me as a four-year-old, which would be the perfect age for me to remember the shape of his face when he smiled. If I could just burn his smile into my memory, then everything would be worth it.

I woke up in the morning to the sight of my beautiful child and gave him a big hug. The morning went great. Breakfast, games… I even let him watch a little TV, just so I could study his face and remember his features as he giggled at his shows. He had fish-sticks for lunch, and as much candy as he wanted once he was done with that.

After lunch, we played with his car collection and then drew pictures. I was so engrossed in what we were doing that I almost didn't even notice when there was movement outside of the living room window. That bastard Gantry was peering inside. I walked over to the door and flung it open, only to see a pale-looking Gantry staring back at me. I started to berate him, "Look here you God damn piece of…" He vomited on my porch before I could finish. I moved my feet to avoid the oncoming flood that was spreading over the ground.

He wiped his face clean with his sleeve. "It's happening again. I can feel it. Whatever it is you're doing, you have to STOP."

"Jeez, don't you have a home? What do I need to do to get rid of you?"

"Just hear me out," he panted. "We figured it out last night. It took some digging and some major hacking, but we know who the waitress is and why she has the Periculo."

"I don't care," I said as I slammed the door shut.

"She's the granddaughter of Tentanum!" he shouted through the door. "She's dangerous!" I didn't respond, and eventually he wandered away from the house when it became clear I wasn't going to engage him any further.

I went back to Fredrick. My time with him was ticking down and I didn't want to let Gantry waste any of it. Whatever concerns he'd raised about Gabriella didn't matter since I wasn't planning on utilizing her services any further. Even I knew when enough was enough.

"Do you want to play a game?' I asked Fredrick.

"Can we play memory?"

"Of course we can," I said. We played, and I rubbed his head and congratulated him when he beat me. But as our games and fun continued, the clock on the wall kept ticking.

As the day wound down, it soon became time for Fredrick's bath, which had always been one of his favorite parts of his day. I set him up in the tub with a whole set of new bath toys that I'd ordered for him. I laughed at how cute he was, splashing around with all of his toys, but my laughter was interrupted when I received a text from Mona—*Emmett is gone! I took a nap, and when I woke up he wasn't in our hotel room. I've been out looking for him, but no luck. I'm really worried.* I nearly responded to her, but I didn't want to give Gantry and his group of hackers anything else to read. Once my day was done, I would go look for him.

Fredrick took a long bath, and when he finally got out, I dressed him in his pajamas. We still had a little time left, so I let him pick out a movie to watch before bed. Then, as we sat down on the couch, I heard a sound in the kitchen—someone was rummaging through one of the drawers. I quickly shot up and darted to the kitchen, cursing the fact that somehow my day with Fredrick was being interrupted yet again. I made it to the kitchen to see Emmett, who'd apparently entered through the back door, holding a steak knife he'd fished from the drawer.

"Whoa, Emmett," I said, trying to calm both him and myself.

Emmett stared straight ahead without any sort of acknowledgement toward me. "No," he said as he shook his head. "No."

"What are you talking about, Emmett?"

"You can't," he said.

Before I could even respond, Emmett lunged at me with surprising speed and strength. Now, I'm a big guy, but somehow Emmett was able to knock me backwards as he ran into the living room. I fell to the floor as I heard Fredrick screaming. In a panic, I righted myself and ran to Fredrick, only to see that Emmett was holding him up with a knife to his throat.

"It's okay, Emmett," I said with a calmness that I didn't truly feel. "Let's get you back home."

Emmett just shook his head. "Don't you feel it? It's not right."

"Emmett, please put the knife down," I pleaded. I could feel the beads of sweat beginning to coalesce on my brow. "That's Fredrick. I know you don't really want to hurt him."

Without another word, Emmett plunged the steak knife into Fredrick's throat as red blood began to flow from the wound. I lunged forward, screaming at Emmett to stop as I collided with both of them. Emmett fell backward to the living room floor as he lost his grasp on Fredrick, who fell onto the couch.

The next few minutes are hard for me to remember. My training kicked in and I switched to autopilot as I tended to Fredrick's wounds. There was a great deal of blood, but I could still feel a strong pulse in his neck. Somewhere along the line I called 911, though I barely recall doing so.

A few minutes later we left in an ambulance, with me by Fredrick's side as the EMTs worked to keep him stable. Meanwhile, I could hear great rumbles of thunder rolling over the sky as lightning flashed through the ambulance windows. The driver couldn't seem to stop commenting on the freaky weather that had appeared out of nowhere. The fact that it was just about time for Fredrick to disappear certainly didn't escape me, yet somehow, he remained—damaged, but present.

Fredrick was admitted to the hospital for overnight observation. Amazingly, his jugular hadn't been severed and a full recovery was expected. There were a ton of questions, of course. I answered them all. Fredrick really shouldn't have been playing with that knife, I told the doctor. It was an awful mistake on my part that wouldn't be repeated. Then I said the same thing to the police officer who responded, and then I said it to the social worker as well. Why they believed me, I don't know, or even really care.

It was morning before I finally started to regain some sense of myself. Even though I'd been awake all night by Fredrick's bedside, I seemed to have a renewed sense of clarity. Fredrick was still with me. For whatever reason, it seemed he had been returned to me for good.

For a while, I didn't even think about the others. Emmett? I'm not even a hundred percent sure what the hell happened to him after I knocked him to the ground. I vaguely remember him somewhat regaining his senses and crawling out of the house before the ambulance got there.

Gabriella? What's left to say about her? I texted her to see if she could shed some light on what the hell was going on. She never wrote back. I visited her restaurant one last time and she wasn't there. She's gone. Who even cares? Once it became clear to me that Fredrick was here to stay, I really didn't need her anyway.

I wish I could say that Gantry disappeared too, but that pencil-necked little bastard showed up again with his same whiny little complaints about the universe being off balance. What does that even mean? One day, not too long after I'd brought Fredrick home from the hospital, I glanced out of my living room window and saw him looking over the fence to my backyard where Fredrick was playing. I went outside and approached him from behind. He was so engrossed in watching Fredrick on his swing set that he didn't even hear me until I cleared my throat and spoke. "If I see you here again, I'll kill you." I had my hands raised up, ready to wrap them around his throat if he said even the slightest wrong thing.

He turned to look at me. "That's not your son," he said.

"Of course that's my son. And I don't want you bothering us any further."

"I finally figured out what you were doing. It's been said that one of the powers of the Hand was bringing back the dead for a day. You used it for your son."

"You and your hacker buddies need to die. Leave us alone." I cracked my knuckles, wanting nothing more than to wrap my hands around his throat and end his life. I probably would've done it if we hadn't been outside in the open.

"You've unleashed something, and you have no idea what you've done. Don't you understand? Your son had to be returned to the past, but his body couldn't be sent back with a stab wound on his neck. Instead, a duplicate was created in his place and only his soul was returned. Meanwhile his broken body stayed here. It was an empty vessel, just waiting for something to inhabit it. And something did. Something got through all the cracks."

I stepped closer to Gantry, my fists clenched and shaking. He understood the threat as he stepped away from the fence. "I'll go if you insist. But just remember, that's not your son. Not anymore. I only wish I could've done something to stop this." He started walking away, but in his typical fashion, he just had to get one more thing in. "Oh, there've been a few murders around here lately." He paused to gauge my reaction, but I gave him nothing. "Do you know how they're related? They were all grandchildren of the people who killed Tentanum." I just stared at him, and that was the end of the conversation. As he walked away, I resisted the urge to reach out and slam him to the ground. I just wanted to get on top of him and strangle him until he was nothing more than a limp sack of blood and bones. It would have felt so good, but I just barely held off this time.

Once I was back inside my living room, I stood there with a smile as I looked outside and watched Fredrick play. He really loved the new swing set I'd bought for him. Next to the swing set stood a brand-new clubhouse that he liked to play in. Next to the clubhouse stood a new climbing structure. And right next to that? That's the spot in the planter bed where we buried the kitten I'd bought for him. Unfortunately, the kitten didn't last more than a day. When I saw Fredrick carrying around its limp body, and I asked him what happened, he just laughed hysterically and then said he'd shaken it too hard. That's okay. I guess he just wasn't ready for that kind of responsibility. I'm sure it was only an accident, and I know he'll be more careful in the future. The important thing is that I have my son back. I WON. I looked the universe in the eye, and the goddam universe blinked. And now, I'll do anything to protect him, to allow him to grow up and reach his full potential, whatever that may be.

FACE DOWN IN THE GRAVE

The corpse of Jeremiah Judson was buried face-down in the grave because he'd been a rotten, no-good asshole and the townspeople thought that it would be the best way to give him one last "fuck you" before sending him off to the ever-after. It hadn't exactly been planned out beforehand, but when the town undertaker mentioned that he'd laid the body face-down in the casket, no one stepped in to complain. On the contrary, the undertaker was applauded and encouraged, and when they held the viewing, most everyone who attended got a good laugh out of seeing Jeremiah's ass facing skyward. In fact, the only reason anyone attended the viewing at all was for the chuckles. Yes, it seemed that everyone had their own personal gripe about the way Jeremiah had conducted himself in life, and not a single one of them was going to step in to stop his unrighteous burial. And that's the story of how Jeremiah went into the ground looking toward Hell.

It wasn't too long before the townspeople realized their mistake—that burying an evil man face down was far worse than burying him face up. Bill Battlings, the undertaker who started the whole thing, was the first one to meet up with an unfortunate accident. An armored car, making its weekly drop-off at the bank, was parked along the side of the road when its doors inexplicably flew open at the same moment that Bill Battlings happened to be walking by. Several heavy bags, filled with quarters, dimes, nickels, and pennies, launched themselves from the car and struck him in the head with enough force to knock him clean out of his shoes and leave a massive dent in his skull. The bags, containing exactly one-thousand dollars of vengeance, left Bill as a wheelchair-bound invalid who spent the rest of his days eating apple sauce and reciting nursery rhymes. The irony of the situation did not escape the townspeople. You see, years earlier Bill had naively loaned a thousand dollars to Jeremiah. Jeremiah, of course, had never bothered to repay the loan while he was still alive.

Others in the town, specifically the ones who'd most enthusiastically encouraged Jeremiah's unholy burial, soon found themselves similarly targeted from beyond. One of those was Gail Gollap, a typically kind lady who ran a café along the town's main thoroughfare. She'd once accused Jeremiah of stealing several hams out of her walk-in refrigerator, which flat-out ruined the Easter dinner service she was planning. Gail unfortunately met her fate about two days after Bill, when she was trampled by a stampede of angry pigs that had somehow broken free from their pen at one of the nearby farms. People couldn't agree on what was more fantastical, the fact that pigs actually stampeded, or the fact that Gail somehow lived through it, losing only her eyesight and hearing.

David Dillinger was next. He was a kindly man who'd been new in town when he hired Jeremiah to help him move furniture into his house. He permanently lost use of his hand when Jeremiah dropped a couch on it. Jeremiah later admitted that he dropped the couch on purpose, just because he thought it would be funny. David, as would be expected, remained bitter about the whole experience, and always saw fit to remind everyone that, however ridiculous it sounded, Jeremiah owed him a new hand. Well, David finally got his wish while he was walking along Main Street and the large sign atop Edna's Glove Shop came loose from the roof and crashed down. The sign, upon which was painted a giant gloved hand, nailed David so hard that when he woke up he couldn't even remember his name, or anything else for that matter. Poor David had to go live in a sanitarium in another town.

It was quickly becoming clear to everybody that Jeremiah Judson was a bigger asshole in death than he'd ever been in life. As more and more people met unfortunate fates, the townsfolk began staying in their homes, fearful of an ironic punishment that they didn't really deserve but would somehow still get. Yes, Jeremiah was in commune with the devil, no doubt brought on by the fact that he was facing straight towards Hell. Had the townsfolk just done the right thing to begin with, maybe Jeremiah would be paying for his own sins, rather than having others do it for him. People argued over the blame, pointing fingers not only at the undertaker but also at those who'd encouraged him, and those who laughed at Jeremiah's butt-up corpse. The one thing they all agreed upon, though, was that Jeremiah needed to be turned around, and fast.

Easy enough, it would seem, to flip a body. Simply dig down, pry the casket open, turn the body over, and rebury. Cal Cooper was the first to try. He marched boldly out to the cemetery, shovel in hand, and started digging. A few adventurous sightseers watched from behind trees, with a healthy dose of fear preventing them from actually helping. They witnessed Cal dig down about two feet before a red lightning bolt pierced the sky and lit him up like a supernova. When he woke up in the hospital a couple of weeks later, he was magnetized and had a difficult time letting go of metal objects. It was only then that Cal remembered that Jeremiah had once stolen electricity from him by patching into his home's electrical panel with a fifty-foot extension cord so that he could watch TV in the van he was living in.

Obviously, Jeremiah liked being face down in the grave, and he liked being an asshole, and it seemed there was nothing anyone could do about it except to wait for their own undeserved ironic comeuppance to be served. It became a chore for everyone to remember all the ways Jeremiah had wronged them, and then try their best to avoid scenarios where it could be used against them. The whole town slowed down and sank into a deep funk.

***

"Wake up!" Francine yelled to her younger brother Fred as she burst into his bedroom. "I'm sick of this shit! We've got to do something."

Fred rubbed his eyes. "What time is it?"

"A quarter 'til six! Time to get moving. We've got a big day."

Fred yawned. "I thought school was canceled."

"It is canceled, but that's not what I'm talking about."

Fred pulled the blanket over his head and tried to go back to sleep. "Whatever it is, do it yourself. I'm sleeping."

"I need you. I can't flip that body all by myself."

Fred shot up. "You can't go out there! Jeremiah's ghost will get you!"

"I've been thinking about this a lot, and you and I never really had a grudge against old Jeremiah, so he has nothing to use against us."

"Yeah, but only because we're just a couple of kids."

"We're not so young anymore, we're teenagers. We can do this. We can save the town."

"What are you going to tell Mom and Dad? That we're just on our way to go dig up some dead guy's body?"

"We're not going to tell them anything," Francine replied, "which is why we need to leave now, before they wake up."

"Yeah, but they'll figure out we're missing soon enough."

"By the time they find us, we'll be done, and we'll be heroes."

Fred rubbed his eyes, still tired and not yet convinced.

Francine studied him. "I'll go alone if I have to," she said.

Fred saw the way his sister's jaw clenched shut and knew she wasn't bluffing. "No, don't go alone. I'll help."

Francine waited while her brother got dressed and ate a quick bowl of cereal. On their way out, they grabbed two shovels and tossed them in the trunk of their father's '57 Suburban. Silently, they pushed the vehicle out of the garage to avoid waking their parents, only starting it once they were halfway down the street. Francine, who had recently turned sixteen and had a brand new driver's license, drove the car.

The day was turning out to be overcast, and a creepy gloominess stayed upon the land far past sunrise. They drove silently to the cemetery, with Francine seeming to have to push harder and harder on the accelerator in order to keep moving forward, as if the car itself didn't particularly want to go to the cemetery. Yet the girl's resolve never faltered, which gave her brother the silent encouragement he needed.

When they arrived a little while later, the morning sunlight still hadn't broken through the clouds, and instead an eerie red glow on the horizon gave the teens barely enough light to see.

They found Jeremiah's gravesite easily enough just by looking for the crater made by Cal Cooper's lightning bolt. They parked the car so that it pointed at the grave, leaving the headlights turned on so that they would have some light to work by.

They both went right to work, not wanting to spend any more time at the cemetery than necessary. Cal's lightning bolt had blasted a good deal of dirt from the site, but even with that head start, the digging was hard work. Their methodical movements were interrupted every so often by the clanking of their shovels banging together, but for the most part they worked very efficiently at digging themselves into a hole.

Rain started at about the time they got waist deep. Heavy drops smacked against their unprotected heads, causing them to periodically stop to brush away the water from their faces. "Keep going," Francine said as she noticed Fred slow his pace. "It's just water." She pulled out a flashlight to help them see in the deepening hole.

Fred redoubled his efforts, and eventually he and his sister both felt their shovels hit the top of Jeremiah's casket. "We're almost there," Francine said. "We just need to widen the hole enough so that we can get the casket open." They worked to clear the dirt away from the top of the casket, with both of them drenched from the rain and their own sweat.

"Okay, I think we have enough room to maneuver," Fred said after a few more minutes. "Let's try to open this thing." He stuck the edge of his shovel under the lid of the casket and began to pry it open. "I hope the body isn't all gross looking."

"Of course it's going to be gross looking. He's been dead for three months. But don't get scared now, we're almost there. We're going to be heroes!" Francine wedged her own shovel underneath the lid and helped her brother pry the lid off. With their combined effort, the lid moved upward with a groan and a creak. "We're doing it!" she said excitedly.

Soon they had the lid pushed up far enough to get a glimpse of the shriveled, gross corpse of Jeremiah Judson. "Ugh, look at that," Fred said. "Let's hurry up and get this over with. We just need to get this lid open a little more." He put his shovel aside and used his hands to try and push the lid all the way open, while Francine focused the beam of her flashlight on the body, still in its prone state. "What's that on his neck?" Fred asked.

Francine moved her head forward to get a better look. "It's his spiderweb tattoo."

Fred looked puzzled for a moment. "You mean that guy with the spiderweb tattoo on his neck was Jeremiah Judson?"

"Yes!" answered Francine.

"I thought Jeremiah was the guy who had the tattoo of a rat on his arm."

"No!" responded Francine. "The guy with the rat tattoo is Harry Hardwick, the town drunk." She pointed at the corpse. "This here is Jeremiah Judson, the town asshole. I mean... how could you not know the difference?"

"I dunno. I'm just a kid."

"Well, you're probably the only person in the whole town who can't tell them apart."

"This might be a problem," Fred said.

"What do you mean?" Francine asked

"It turns out I DO have a grudge against this guy. He destroyed my entire collection of toy cars."

"What are you talking about?"

"Remember when I was outside playing with all my cars, and then some guy drove down the street and veered onto our lawn and ran over all of them, then laughed and drove off? He owes me some cars!"

"You told Mom and Dad that it was Harry Hardwick who did that."

"Yeah, that's because I thought Harry was the one with the spiderweb tattoo."

As if on cue, the headlights of the car went dark, while at the same time Francine's flashlight suddenly extinguished, leaving the children in near total darkness. Only the tiniest bit of noon sunlight managed to penetrate through the gloomy storm clouds. "What just happened?" Fred asked. "I can't see what I'm doing."

Francine shook her flashlight. No luck. "Give me a boost out of here. I'll go check on the headlights."

Fred laced the fingers of his hands together and leaned down so that Francine could step into his palms and get a boost. With an oomph, he lifted his sister out of their hole. "Now pull me up," he said as his sister righted herself.

"Hold on," she said. "Let me just go check on the lights real fast."

As Francine stepped away from the grave, the car's engine unexpectedly turned over, and a moment later it lurched forward with a groan as it strained against its own parking brake. Francine dove out of the way as it rolled past her toward the open grave.

Seeing this, Fred decided immediately that he didn't need help to get out of the grave after all. He jumped up and grabbed onto the edge of the hole and almost managed to pull himself out, right up to the point where he felt a hand wrap around his ankle and yank him back down into the hole. "He's got me! He's got me!" he screamed as he collapsed back down.

Francine's jaw dropped as she watched the car close in on the open grave where her brother was stuck. She got back up from the ground and rushed over to the car that was still creeping its way along. Flinging the door open, she sat in the driver's seat and jammed her foot on the brake, causing the car to come to a stop just a couple of feet from the opening. Francine wiped the rain and sweat away from her face as she said a small thank you. But her gratitude was too early. The weight of the car, perched so close to the edge of the grave, caused the wet dirt to start caving in on her brother.

The car, or whatever was controlling it, seemed to sense that its target was within reach. The engine revved higher, with the sound from the engine overpowering the crashing of the rain. The tires, unable to gain traction, began to spin in place, churning up mud and eating away at the edge of the hole. Francine tried to put the car into reverse, but the controls would no longer respond to her as the car scraped itself deeper into the grave, trying to reach its prey huddled at the bottom.

It soon became apparent, though, that the spinning wheels could only do so much digging, and that the boy at the bottom of the semi-collapsed hole was relatively safe for the time being. The car's horn honked in frustration as the wheels flew into reverse, spinning in place for a brief moment until the tires finally found enough traction. At that point, the whole car lurched backwards to the same spot where it had been parked earlier. The engine, however, remained running, as if it was just waiting for Fred to poke his head out of the grave.

Francine flung the door open and carefully inched her way to the edge of the grave. Much of the surrounding mud had collapsed into the hole, and she had to be careful that she herself didn't fall in. She saw that Jeremiah's corpse had been completely covered up, while Fred was buried up to his waist in mud. Looking at her brother, Francine judged that the car's tires must've gotten to within a couple of inches of his face. If it had managed to get any closer, the left side of Fred's head would've been ground meat.

"Get me out of here!" he screamed. He tried lifting his legs out of the mud. "I swear I can feel his hand wrapped around my ankle."

Francine gave a hesitant glance back toward the idling car before lowering herself into the hole. She fished around in the dirt, looking for their two shovels and seeing them both right next to each other. "Here. Start digging," she said as she wrenched them loose from the mud and handed one of them to Fred. He immediately began scraping away at the mud that covered his legs, and with the help of his sister, most of the mud was soon moved aside. As soon as he could move, Fred wrenched his legs free and began to clamor up the side of the grave.

"No," Francine said as she pulled him back by the shoulder. "We've come too far to give up. And anyway, you're a sitting duck if you go out there. That car is waiting for you."

"Did you hear what I said? Jeremiah's corpse grabbed my ankle and pulled me back down here. I'd rather take my chances up there with Dad's car than down here with the body."

"We've come too far and gone through too much to quit now. Let's keep digging."

"Yeah, but there's still no light," Fred said, still looking for an excuse to leave.

"We'll just have to do our best without it. We don't need light to know how to dig downward." She pushed her shovel into the mud, starting the process of uncovering Jeremiah's body once again.

Spurred on by his sister's bravery, Fred started digging alongside her. The work was exhausting, but eventually the two of them nearly uncovered the casket for a second time, and as Francine heaved the last few shovels full of dirt over her shoulder, Fred stood ready in a defensive stance with his shovel held in front of him, lest Jeremiah's corpse start moving around. When the last bit of dirt was cleared away, Francine pried open the casket fully. She could just barely make out the shape of the body, which remained motionless, with one of its arms positioned outward, as if it was reaching for something.

"See?" Fred said as he pointed at the corpse's outstretched arm. "It DID grab me." He poked at the body with a shovel, seeing if it would react, but it remained motionless.

"C'mon," Francine said as she reached down to try and lift the body. "If you don't want to help me lift, then at least use your shovel to clear some of this mud out of the casket." Fred did as he was directed as Francine reached in and pulled the body upward. With limited room to move around in the hole, she struggled to reposition the corpse so that it could be laid on its back. "There's not... enough... room," she grunted. "I hate to say this, but one of us has to get out of here."

"I'll go," Fred volunteered. "I'm pretty sure that thing just winked at me."

Francine paused for a moment to contemplate the situation. "Okay, but keep an eye on Dad's car. Until I get Jeremiah put back in the casket correctly, anything can happen." She stood high and craned her neck out of the hole to survey their surroundings. "Once you're out, make a dash for that tree over there. It looks sturdy. Keep it between you and the car." Francine laced up her hands so that she could give her brother a boost out of the hole. "Once you're out, just make a run for it. Don't hesitate!"

Fred nodded and allowed Francine to boost him up and out of the hole. He glanced cautiously at the car as he pulled himself up, and then began backing away from it, keeping it in his field of view. As soon as he took his third step back, the car lurched forward. "Shit!" Fred screamed as he turned and started running for the tree. "Maybe I should've been the one to stay in the hole."

Francine, who was struggling to get the corpse in the casket correctly, heard the revving engine and peaked her head out of the hole, only to witness Fred trying his best to run toward the tree. The car spun its wheels in pursuit, and most likely would've caught up to Fred if not for the soppy mud that slowed its acceleration.

"No!" Francine yelled as she released her grip on the corpse. Using every last ounce of her strength, she pulled herself from the hole and tried to chase after the car, desperately hoping that she could jump inside and stop it one more time, but it was simply too far ahead for her to even try that. However, she gave a quick sigh of relief as Fred made it successfully to the tree, diving behind it. Her delight was quick-lived, however, as she saw that the car didn't even slow down, and instead plowed into the tree with one final growl from its engine.

The tree proved to be weaker than Francine had anticipated, and gave way to the car that had just smashed into it. With a giant groan, the tree leaned over, then slowly began toppling toward the ground. Fred scrambled to get out of its way, taking a few steps before slipping in the mud and falling face down. The tree collapsed, and its heavy branches fanned out and pinned Fred to the ground. The car's engine sputtered and then died out.

Francine ran over to Fred and kneeled beside him. "Are you okay?"

Fred opened his eyes. "Am I dead?"

Francine ran her eyes over Fred from head to toe. Despite being pinned down, he seemed to be okay. "You're not dead," she answered. "Can you get out from under there? Here, let me try to move this branch off of you."

Fred pushed back at the branches that were holding him down and began to extract himself from underneath the tree, but a lightning flash, which illuminated the whole cemetery, caused him to stop cold. "Look!" he said to his sister as he pointed back toward the grave with a shaky arm.

Francine turned around to see what Fred was pointing at, only to be confronted with the sight of Jeremiah Judson standing outside of his grave, looking at the siblings.

With a final push, Fred freed himself from under the last of the branches. "Let's get out of here!" he said. "While we still have a chance."

"No," Francine replied as she stood up and faced toward Jeremiah, whose corpse stood silently at the edge of his grave. "We need to finish what we started. We've unleashed something, and I think if we leave now, things might even get worse for this town."

"Look at that! There's nothing else we can do."

"No. I'm not going to be afraid. In fact, I may even have the advantage."

"What are you talking about?"

Francine didn't answer. She just stood in the rain, staring at Jeremiah, whose sunken yellow eyes stared right back at her from across the graveyard. She stepped boldly through the mud as the head on Jeremiah's corpse slowly turned to keep her in its sight. She kept walking until she was standing right in front of him. The corpse raised its hands, as if it was contemplating choking all of the life from Francine.

"You have no power over me," she said boldly. "Do you remember me?"

Jeremiah's head moved back and forth as if to say no.

"I'm not surprised. Let me refresh your memory. Do you remember the day when you stole a horse, and you rode it through the park, and the horse got spooked and kicked over Dot Dodgeson's ice cream cart?"

The rain continued to fall while Jeremiah just stared back at Francine.

"But then you saw a little girl who'd fallen from the monkey bars in all the commotion, so you got off the horse and walked over to that little girl. Then you held out your hand and helped the little girl get back up onto her feet."

Jeremiah's corpse nodded as the memory came back.

"Well, Jeremiah, I was that little girl. When you helped me up, that was an act of kindness, probably the only one of your entire life."

Jeremiah pointed at the girl.

"Yes, it was me. You helped me up from the ground when I fell."

The earth under Jeremiah's feet suddenly cracked open and then gave way entirely, spilling into the grave and taking Jeremiah along with it. Francine, who jumped backwards to avoid the sliding mud, heard a thud as the body landed back inside its open casket. Once the ground stopped shifting, she took a cautious step forward and saw that the corpse of Jeremiah Judson was lying perfectly still, face up in the grave.

Fred, who'd been watching from afar, stepped up to the grave in amazement. "How did you do that? Are you some sort of witch or something?"

"No," Francine replied matter-of-factly, "I just figured that if people were being punished for all the bad things that Jeremiah did to them, then maybe I would be rewarded for the one nice thing he did for me."

Fred smiled. "It sounds like you just got really lucky."

Francine shrugged. "Maybe, or it might be that I'm smart."

Fred shook his head and retrieved a shovel. "Okay smarty-pants, let's finish this."

Up in the sky, the rain clouds began to part as the afternoon sun began to shine down on the cemetery. Jeremiah's corpse felt the momentary pleasure of the warm sun upon its face, while at the same time the pain of burning hell-fire slowly began creeping up along its back. Seconds later, the lid was put back on the coffin, and for Jeremiah, it was dark.

The two took their time to finish the job, completely filling in the grave with the dirt they'd excavated. "You think he's gone for good?" Fred asked.

"Yep," Francine replied. "The only thing we have to worry about now is trying to explain to Dad what happened to his car."

Fred used his shovel to pat down the last bit of dirt over the grave. "Yeah, I think we killed the car, but maybe Dad will go easy on us because, well, we saved the town."

"Let's hope so," Francine said with a laugh. With that, the siblings began their walk back home, stopping only to admire the beautiful rainbow that had formed in the sky.

TAFFY BOMB

When Marcus and Jesse went trick-or-treating, a human-sized rat answered the door at the very first house they went to. This was not an adult dressed up in a costume, as one might first suspect, but an actual huge rat that stood on its two hind legs and sneered wickedly at both of the boys.

"Trick-or-tre..." Jesse's voice faded off as he took in the sight of the giant rat standing in front of him. The creature was disgusting, and the shape of its body was unlike anything any man could contort himself into. The rat snarled as he shot out a pair of stubby hands, digging his claws deep into Jesse's arms and yanking him into the house.

Marcus, the older of the two boys, screamed out in panic, "Hey let my brother go!" He darted inside the house, following the giant rat as it dragged Jesse into the living room.

The rat flung the younger boy to the floor like a sack of potatoes and then turned to face Marcus. "Stop!" the rat commanded in a snarling voice as he held up his paw. "That's close enough." The rat dropped down onto all four legs and scurried over to where he'd tossed Jesse, placing a paw upon the boy's throat. It was then that Marcus saw the extra sharp sets of claws emanating from each of the rat's paws. A slight trickle of blood ran down Jesse's throat as the rat's dirty claw started to push deeper into it. "Come any closer and this boy's throat will be shredded."

Marcus stopped instantly. "Please don't hurt him. He's only seven."

The rat sized-up Marcus, who was much bigger than his brother. "How old are you?" he asked.

Marcus gulped, but still managed to answer. "Thirteen."

"Hmm," said the rat, "almost a little too old to be trick-or-treating."

"My mom has to work late, so if I didn't go there would be nobody to take my brother."

"Actually, I think you being older will work out a little better," said the rat, deep in contemplation. "Now listen up, because if you do as I say, I won't hurt him."

Marcus looked on as the rat stood back up on its hind legs. It was a very unnatural-looking creature—its body seemed to be purely animal, but its face was a fusion of rat and human elements, with an insignificant snout and perfectly human teeth to go along with beady eyes and rat ears. It gave off the impression that maybe, long ago, the rat had been fully human.

"What do you want?" Marcus asked with a quivering voice.

"I want the same thing anyone else wants on this night. Candy."

Marcus held up his empty bag. "I don't have any."

"Well, you don't have any yet, but that will change soon. Put down that tiny bag of yours and grab that bag over there," the rat commanded as he pointed to a large black bag on the floor. "Go trick-or-treating and fill it up. ALL THE WAY UP. Then bring it back to me. If you have enough to tip the scales, then you will have succeeded."

"Scales?"

The rat pointed to the corner where an old dusty balance scale sat on the floor. One of the plates had a pair of iron dumbbells perched atop of it. The opposite plate was empty. "You put your candy here," said the rat as it stepped over to the scales and pointed at the empty plate. "And if you have enough, the scale will tip in your favor, and you and your brother will go home safe."

Marcus looked at the dumbbells. Each one was marked with a "25" on the side. "I need to bring back fifty pounds of candy?" he asked.

The rat nodded. "Yes. It's still early, so you might have enough time if you leave now. You have until midnight."

Marcus turned to Jesse, who was sprawled on the floor, too afraid to move or talk. "Don't worry Jesse. I promise you'll be safe."

Jesse nodded in acknowledgment.

With shaky hands, Marcus grabbed the bag he'd been instructed to use and walked backwards toward the front door, not letting the rat or Jesse out of his sight until the last possible moment. As he exited the house through the open door, he could see the rat poke its head through the blinds of the front window, watching him. He was in a neighborhood he wasn't completely familiar with, having gone there after hearing talk from the other kids about all the great candy that got passed out. His unfamiliarity with the area only added to his fear as he took a moment to contemplate his situation.

He had no intention of doing the rat's bidding, but since he was clearly being observed, he felt it would be better to at least put on a show until he got far enough away so that he could call the police, lest he endanger his brother.

He walked up to the next-door house and rang the bell. "Trick or treat," his wavering voice said as the door opened.

A woman in a princess costume greeted him. "Oh, look at you," she said, admiring his vampire outfit. She reached into a bowl and grabbed a few candies, placing them in Marcus's bag while his eyes nervously shifted to the rat's house.

"Thank you," he said. He made it back to the sidewalk and looked down the street. Seven more houses and he'd be to the last house on the block. He figured that would be the safest place to stop and call the police. He made his way there, slowly but surely trick-or-treating at each house along the way and doing his best to act natural.

When he finally reached the last house on the block, he didn't even wait for the door to be fully opened before he started begging for help. "Please, I need you to call the police! My little brother has been kidnapped! He's being held in a house just down the street."

The old man who answered the door just smiled. "Oh, you kids and your little pranks." He held a bowl of candy out toward Marcus. "Help yourself."

"No! You don't understand. It's not a prank. Please call the police."

The old man's smile faltered. He looked around to see if there was anyone else outside of his house. "Look, if you don't want any candy, then it's probably best you leave. I don't want any part of your shenanigans."

Marcus became desperate. "Call the goddam police! Please!" It was then that he noticed the rats that had begun congregating on the porch alongside him. Out from the bushes and crevices they crawled—these were common rats, not like the nasty human-sized rat that held his brother, but what they lacked in size they made up for in numbers.

The old man went from confused to angry when he saw all the rats starting to pile up on his porch. "What's the meaning of this?" he asked. "I told you I don't want any part of your Halloween shenanigans!" He tried to close the door, but the rats began pushing themselves inside and started crawling up his pant legs. "Hey stop them!" he screamed out as he fell to the ground. The rats dog-piled on top of the defenseless man and began biting him aggressively, tearing away his flesh as he screamed out in pain. On the street, the other trick-or-treaters commented on how realistic the screams sounded, not even for a moment considering that they were anything other than a special effect from someone's decorations.

The rats dragged the old man inside even as they kept eating his flesh. The door slammed closed behind them and the porch light somehow turned off. Soon the man's screams got fainter and then stopped altogether. Back on the porch, a couple of pumpkins that had been alight suddenly extinguished on their own. Marcus stood alone in the darkness.

His next thought was to turn and run home—his mom would be getting home from work eventually. She'd believe him, but the thought of her possibly getting eaten by rats too caused him to reconsider. Instead, he did the only thing that seemed logical to him—he kept on trick-or-treating.

He moved over to the next street, passing up slower-moving trick-or-treaters and going from house to house as quickly as possible. All the while, he noticed rats watching him, poking their little heads out from behind fences and crawling down from trees as he approached. Some followed him, apparently keeping tabs on what he was doing, while others simply stared as he walked by. They made him very uneasy.

He couldn't help but wonder if he would even have enough time to get all the candy he needed. He reached into his bag and pulled out a fun-size candy bar. The nutrient label on the back said it weighed half an ounce. The wheels and cogs of his quick, analytical mind began turning as he crunched the numbers in his head. His face fell as he calculated his final result—he would need to collect over 1,600 pieces of candy, and that was only if all the other candies were as big as the candy bar in his hand, which most probably were not.

He decided he needed to be more demanding, and he started asking people in the houses for more candy, even after they'd given him a handful. Sometimes it worked, and sometimes people told him not to be greedy before slamming their door shut. He doubled back on a few of the houses that were giving away full-sized candy bars, hoping that the residents either wouldn't notice or wouldn't care that he'd already been there. He was especially blessed when he got to the big yellow house with the white trim. The lady there was giving away taffy bombs that were as big as lemons and just as heavy. Another house had an unattended bowl of candy sitting out with a note saying, "take one." Marcus dumped the whole bowl into his bag and made a silent apology to whoever might be upset by his actions.

The night wore on and the black bag began getting heavy. As he wound his way through the various neighborhoods, his breathing became labored and raspy. Eventually, the impossibility of his task became apparent as more and more porch lights were being turned off. It seemed many of the townsfolk didn't want to stay up too late. He had made significant headway, but he was smart enough to know that with his opportunities dwindling, he would likely come up short. He had to think of a plan... he knew Thompson's General Store would still be open, and it wasn't that far away. They sold all sorts of candy there. Maybe... just maybe...

He glanced around—it seemed as if the rats had become bored with him in the hours since he'd first started trick-or-treating, and he didn't see any in the immediate vicinity. He walked purposefully and calmly to a row of hedges, under which he quickly stowed his bag of candy. He walked down the street to the end of the cul-de-sac where a cinderblock wall separated the neighborhood from the city streets beyond.

He jumped and pulled himself up and over the wall, dropping down to the sidewalk below a moment later. Not wasting any time, he jogged until he reached the General Store a few minutes later. As he neared, he found himself bathed in the warm glow of the huge sign atop the building that said, *"Thompson's General Store"* in bold letters. Underneath, their tagline read, *"We Sell Everything You Need."* The automatic doors slid open as he stepped inside and grabbed a basket. He went right to the candy aisle and saw that it was mostly picked over. Still, there was enough left over to make his trip worthwhile. He scooped up nearly all the candy that was left and dropped it into his basket, then went to the register.

The clerk greeted him and then slowly began punching each item into the register. About halfway through, he looked up to see Marcus's desperate and sad eyes. "You okay?" the clerk asked.

Marcus silently nodded his head, fearful that an army of rats would come bursting into the store if he did anything else.

The clerk finished his tally. "That'll be nineteen dollars and fifty cents."

Marcus pulled his wallet from his pocket and counted the money out. "Thank you," he said as he grabbed his bag of candy. He said a little prayer under his breath that he would have enough, and jogged back to collect his Halloween bag, finding it right where he'd stashed it. He added his new haul to the bag and began retracing his path back to the home where the rat was. It wasn't an easy journey with his huge bag of candy, and he arrived at the home sweaty and shaky from the effort. The porch was still dark, but Marcus, who was determined to save his brother, marched right up and knocked on the door.

The door opened, seemingly on its own, and Marcus stepped inside.

"Good, you're back," he heard the rat say. "Come closer, and set your bag down on the scale."

Marcus stepped into the living room, where he saw Jesse sitting in a corner, surrounded by a group of rats. His eyes were open, but he seemed to be staring out into space, as if he was in some sort of trance. Marcus placed the bag on the scale and watched as it slowly tipped in his favor. "Can I have my brother back now?" he asked. "It looks like there's enough."

The rat jammed its paw into the bag and pulled out a few candies and studied them carefully. "There's something wrong," he said as he kicked the bag off the scale and onto its side, spilling the candies onto the floor. "Some of these candies have not been properly attained." He picked up one of the store-bought candies and smelled it. "Garbage!" he said as he flung it into the next room. "Did you buy these at a store?"

Marcus just stood silently.

The rat sifted through the candies, angrily identifying and picking out the rejects. "Don't you understand, you foolish boy?" he said without even looking up. "The only candies I'm interested in are the ones that have been obtained under threat. THAT'S what places a hallowed mark upon them! If you didn't say trick-or-treat to get them then I can't use them. If it was as simple as going to the store, I wouldn't need to use rotten children such as you."

The exasperated rat fell to its bottom. "And I had such hope for you." The rat shifted his focus to the candies on the floor, when all of the sudden his gaze was drawn directly to the taffy bomb that Marcus had collected earlier in the evening. "I haven't seen one of these before," he said as he lifted it up to his face.

"It's a taffy bomb," Marcus said. "One of the shops in town makes them. A house on the next street is giving them away."

The rat took the paper wrapper off and tossed the giant candy in its mouth, chewing twice before swallowing it. "Not bad," he said. "Might even be the best candy I've eaten in the last ten years." The rat looked at Marcus as if he had just noticed that he was still there. "You wasted time with your cheating, but you still have until midnight."

Marcus grabbed the now-empty bag and headed backed toward the front door, taking one last look at his catatonic brother. "I'll be back, Jesse. I promise you'll be safe."

***

Late. It was getting far too late. Many of the houses had shut their lights off and were obviously no longer handing out candy. Marcus ran between the few houses that were still available, rudely asking for extra candy if he saw that people still had more to give. He went to houses multiple times, especially those that gave away the full-size candies, frantically tiring himself out until, one by one, the residents either yelled at him for being such a greedy young man or simply stopped answering their doors. He made it back to the yellow house with the white trim one more time before they too turned off their light.

He somehow managed to get a respectable amount of candy, but eventually, the streets became completely dark as the rest of the houses shut their lights off and the last of the die-hard trick-or-treaters retreated back to their homes. He was alone in the dark, and his vampire costume did little to shield him from the cold air that seemed to be seeping up from the ground. The rats had returned as well. He couldn't see them, but the sound of their shuffling feet and their faint squeaks told him they were nearby, watching him.

He wanted to just leave—to go to his own home, crawl into bed, and pretend that everything was fine, but he'd made a promise to Jesse. Nearly a mile away, he could see the lights of Thompson's General Store creating an aura on the horizon. They wouldn't be open too much longer. He glanced into his bag of candy, and then, believing that he wouldn't have enough, he ditched it behind a tree and ran back to the store in one final, desperate move.

He barely made it to the general store before it closed. In fact, the clerk was locking the front doors when Marcus arrived, but he was nice enough to let him inside, as long as he promised to be fast.

"I'll be quick," Marcus agreed.

***

Marcus struggled back to the rat's house, wearily dragging his bag on the ground behind him. He knocked on the door, which opened with a low-pitched creak. He was out of breath, out of time, and nearly out of hope. He took a deep breath and entered.

"What do you have for me?" the rat asked.

Marcus dropped the bag down to the floor and pointed to it.

"You went back to the store again, didn't you?" the rat asked.

"Yes," Marcus admitted, "but they were all out of candy by the time I got there."

The rat stuck its head in the bag. "Well, it appears to be in order. They all have the hallowed mark." He glared at Marcus suspiciously. "Put it on the scale."

Marcus saw that the rat had taken the time to separate the candy he'd dropped off earlier, with the trick-or-treated candy piled upon the scale and the store-bought candy strewn about the room. Marcus stepped up to the scale and began adding the new candy from his bag. Handful after handful he added, until he reached in and grabbed his final bit and placed it on the scale, praying that it would be enough to put him over. The scale wobbled momentarily, causing both Marcus and the rat to gasp, but in the end it refused to tip.

"You failed, boy. Now both you and your brother will become rat food. However, I admit you did well. I've never had anyone come this close. I'll make sure the rats give you a quick death."

"Wait!" yelled Marcus. "I have one more piece of candy." He reached inside and pulled out what truly was the last item in the bag, another taffy bomb. He reached out and placed it atop the pile of sweets. The candy plate moved slowly downward, while the plate with the weights shifted upward. Marcus and all the rats watched in silent anticipation…

But it was not to be, despite its momentary flirt with gravity, the candy plate wasn't quite heavy enough to move all the way down, and it soon floated back upward, just a mere ounce shy of its goal.

Marcus began to scream in protest. The rat, after all, had already eaten the first taffy bomb that he'd brought, and had that been added to the total, he would've succeeded. The rat didn't listen though, and Marcus's objections were quickly silenced by the rats that came scurrying out of their crevices and immediately began climbing up his clothing. They reached his throat and tore their way through it so quickly that he was dead before his body even hit the ground—quick, just as the rat had promised.

The big rat looked at his feasting minions and actually felt some degree of admiration for their victim. That boy had been smart and resourceful, but his admiration lasted only a moment as he shifted his attention to the nearly fifty pounds of authentic Halloween candy in front of him. What a haul! This would easily last him a year, enabling him to cast spells and charms all the way through until the next Halloween, when he would travel to some other town and start all over again.

He made a mental note that in future years he would have to demand more than fifty pounds. The last thing he wanted was to have a kid succeed in the task, and this particular kid had come too damn close. He shuddered at the thought of having to choose between actually letting a victim go free, or suffering the bad fortune that would go along with killing someone who'd been successful in the challenge.

Then, his thought process faltered, with his attention being diverted to the big taffy bomb that was perched atop his pile of candy. It looked especially delicious to him. He shooed away his rat minions, who were eagerly looking for a piece of enchanted tribute for their night's work. "No," he told them as they sniffed at the taffy bomb. "It's mine, and you can't have it! It's been a long night and I need to recharge my powers." His greedy paw shot forward and grabbed it away from the rats before they could get it. He unwrapped the delicious confectionary and popped the whole thing in his gaping mouth. It was nearly as delicious as the first one, but slightly different.

Suddenly, he felt a sharp pain in his abdomen as his stomach began to gurgle. Something was seriously wrong. He licked his chops, trying to figure out the intricate flavors of the taffy bomb as his stomach rumbled. He tasted strawberry, cream, vanilla, and… something not so good.

The giant rat fell face-down, right next to the newly skeletonized body of Marcus. He crawled along the floor with no real destination in his mind. How could he have missed it? His last thought, before fully succumbing, was a grudging respect for Marcus. As soon as his final breath left his lungs, his rat minions all started screaming, as if each and every last one of them was being tortured to death. The screaming rats, those who were in the house and those who were spread about town, all reached an ear-piercing crescendo before they too fell dead.

Jesse, free of his catatonic state, fell into a deep slumber. As promised, he was safe.

Across town, the night clerk at Thompson's General Store was busy finishing up the last of his nightly chores before heading home. It had been an odd shift, with the only customer being the young man who had first come by to buy candy, and then came back at closing to buy rat poison. "There must be an interesting story behind that," he mused as he turned off the lights and left the store. And with that, the last of the town fell into a peaceful darkness.

DECAMONOPROGENY

The demon was trapped in the room and couldn't escape as long as someone was sitting in front of the doorway. The problem was, there had to be someone there all day, every day, and demonsitter isn't exactly the type of job you could advertise for on the internet. Could you even imagine what an ad like that would look like?

Help wanted! Join our dynamic team of pious, stodgy laypeople who've maintained a decades-long vigil over a powerful, evil being who enjoys destroying souls. Must be good at resisting psychological games, spiritual attacks, and invasive mind probing. Pay is nearly non-existent, but a monthly stipend will be provided to those who last that long. Please inquire within for this exciting opportunity to help keep this captured demon off the streets!

So I'm sure you can understand that finding someone to fill a position like that wouldn't be easy. And yet, for a long time (decades actually), three dedicated people worked in twelve-hour shifts, keeping a never-ending watch upon the captured hell-spawn. Over the years, other watchers stepped in and tried to help out, but none of them lasted long. It was the same core-three who kept coming back, but they were getting old—their minds were becoming faulty, and their bodies were getting achy. The cracks were showing, and a new generation of dedicated watchers, ones who could withstand the demon's attacks, was needed.

So why did the congregation choose me to help them? Because I was a lifelong member of the church who was willing, faithful, and available. I'd spent many of my formative years as part of the church's youth group and had forged some meaningful friendships. I owed so much to the congregation. I'll admit, I tried to talk my way out of it after I'd already accepted the job and then came to understand what it entailed. "I didn't realize this is a real-life demon," I argued. "I mean, growing up I heard the rumors like everyone else, but... I'm not qualified for this kind of thing."

"Nobody is qualified for this," came Pastor Johansson's the terse reply. I couldn't argue with that logic.

I was given several days of instruction before I was to start, but for the most part, what they taught me all boils down to the following points:

- Do not touch the demon.
- Do not leave the room until relieved.
- There can be only one person in the room at a time with the demon, otherwise one of them will be manipulated into injuring or killing the other. I guess they found this out the hard way.
- The demon is stuck in a corporeal state, but its physical appearance will be different every time you see it.
- The demon can't physically hurt you while you are in the room.
- Your best bet is to just ignore it, if you can.
- Again, do not touch the demon.

On my first night, I arrived at the church and then forced my quivering legs to carry me toward the dark staircase that would take me down to the musty basement. A heavy wooden door greeted me when I got to the bottom. I took a deep breath and knocked three times. The door creaked open and I was greeted by an elderly, tired looking gentleman named Eldon, whom I'd met a few times during my training. He gave a smile when he saw me. "Good evening, Bennet," he said. He glanced at my shaky hands and added, "You're going to do fine."

I nodded and put one foot inside the room, as I'd been instructed. He then stepped one foot outside of the room so that we were both half in and half out. "Ready?" he asked. I nodded, and then we both picked up our remaining feet, so that as he completely left the room, I entered it. The solid door creaked closed behind me. The only lighting was from a single, flickery overhead fluorescent tube, but it was enough for me to see just how dingy and dusty my surroundings were. The walls and ceiling had large, dark splatters on them. Blood? I wasn't sure. The room smelled damp and dirty. I don't know why I was surprised by the state of the room—it's not like you could just bring a cleaning crew in to spruce everything up.

There was a single chair for me to sit in, right next to the door. The demon was huddled in the corner. It was the size of a child, but its face was wrinkled and withered. Its gray hair grew greasy and long. After a few uneasy moments, the thing spoke to me. "Will you help me?" it said in a surprisingly sweet voice.

I'd been told to expect such things and knew better than to answer.

"I'm in a lot of pain."

I sat down in the chair and looked at my watch. Eleven hours and fifty-nine minutes to go.

"I'd like to go to a hospital." The demon held up an arm that had an unnatural bend in it, as if it had a broken bone. "See?"

Eleven hours and fifty-eight minutes to go. I shifted my gaze away.

The demon slowly stepped closer to me and smiled. "You would ignore a little old person in need?" it asked incredulously. Then it laughed as it dropped all pretense. Its voice suddenly took a commanding tone. "You are Bennet Melton. Twenty-six years old. You're an only child and you live with your mother. She thinks you're working here as a janitor because you didn't think she'd believe the truth. Graduated college two years ago with a degree in sociology, but you still haven't found a job yet. You've been drunk only once in your life. Virgin—not by choice, although you pretend that it is. You always wear long sleeve shirts because you don't want people to see your arms." The demon gave a knowing wink.

I instinctively tugged on my sleeves. My life story sounded sad when distilled down to such basic elements. No matter. I remained stoic.

"You're a loser, Bennet. You've got no future, at least not one that you'll look back on in your old age and be proud of. You should leave here with me, and together we'll go out and paint the town red."

I remained silent.

"Talk to me, Bennet. Things will be so much more interesting if you talk." The demon continued to stare at me, leaning in so that it was only inches from my face. I could feel the short puffs of its breath drumming against my cheek. "I can do this... forever," it said.

I managed to ignore the unmoving creature for hours, and even became accustomed to the smell of its breath, which oddly smelled of roses. But I had my limits, and eventually I broke down and spoke. "Stop it," I demanded.

The demon backed up as a cackle erupted from its throat. "You broke way too fast. I was right about you. You're a loser."

"You know nothing about me. You're nothing more than a liar!" I shot back, knowing full well that simply by speaking, I'd been bested.

"Oh, make no mistake, I'm unrivaled among all liars. But the very best liars tell the truth nearly all of the time, and you know full well that nothing I've said tonight is a lie."

I turned away again, this time with renewed strength, determined not to speak. The withered demon giggled and walked back to the corner of the room, where it sat down on the floor. For the rest of that night, nothing more was said, but that damn thing never took its eyes off me.

***

I returned the next night, feeling as if I'd rather be anywhere else. I checked in with Pastor Johansson before I started my shift. "Last night was incredibly difficult. Even harder than I was expecting," I said.

He nodded his head in understanding. "This is the most important thing you'll ever do. It'll get easier with time. I promise."

"But how long does that take?" I asked.

The pastor looked almost annoyed. "I don't know. It just takes time."

"During my training, Eldon mentioned that you used to cover shifts for them, but not anymore. Why is that?"

"There are very good reasons. I won't go into them now."

"But you still expect others to go?"

"... yes."

The pastor's answers left me wholly unsatisfied, nonetheless I persisted. "Why is that thing even here? Shouldn't you have important people dealing with something of this magnitude?"

"We're a lone congregation. We're the ones who trapped the demon, and the obligation to guard it falls upon us, and only us."

***

I strode crossly toward the basement and descended the staircase. I'm not sure what I'd been expecting to get out of my conversation with the pastor, but whatever it was, I hadn't gotten it. I put my reservations aside and knocked three times on the door. Eldon let me in with a pleasant greeting and I switched places with him. I was immediately greeted by a horrible sight. This time, instead of a small, wrinkled being, a monstrous form stood in front of me in full demon regalia—warts all over its skin, horns coming from its head, misshapen joints, jagged teeth. The thing must've stood seven feet tall. It was almost as if the demon was going intentionally overboard in its attempt to unsettle me, and it worked. I thought back to what I was told in training to help calm myself—The demon cannot physically harm you while you're in the room.

I sat on the chair and looked to the ground. The demon resumed its staring game from the night before, but this time I could feel it penetrating my thoughts. "You brought a book with you tonight. Are you going to read me some stories?" it asked with a baritone voice.

I'd brought a small bible with me, stuffed into my pants pocket. It had belonged to my father.

"Did you really think that would help you?" the demon asked. It moved closer, with its face only inches from mine. Its breath smelled of rotten fish. "The Bible is one of my favorite books. Will you read it to me?"

My hands clenched together until my knuckles were white.

The demon chuckled. "You brought that book because you believe it will give you protection, and now that I ask you to read it to me, you remain silent? You must not have much faith after all."

I reached into my pocket, pulled the Bible out, and opened it to the New Testament.

"No. The Old Testament is far more interesting. Read 2 Kings 2:23," the demon said.

I ignore the request and started reading the verse I wanted, "God made him who had no sin to be sin for us, so that in him we might become the righteousness of God..."

"Read me what I asked for," the demon interrupted. "Or are you afraid that there are certain parts of the Bible that won't hold up?"

I paused, then flipped to the Old Testament and read the requested passage. "Elisha left Jericho to go to Bethel, and on the way some boys came out of a town and made fun of him. 'Get out of here, baldy!' they shouted. Elisha turned around, glared at them, and cursed them in the name of the LORD. Then two she-bears came out of the woods and tore forty-two of the boys to pieces..." my voice trailed off.

The demon roared in laughter to the point where it actually fell down and rolled on the ground. "See?" it said between fits of laughter. "Once you get past all the dry parts, that book is hilarious!"

"You can't take that literally," I said. "You have to understand the implications. They weren't just a group of simple children. They were a gang of evil young men who found themselves judged by God for threatening his prophet."

The demon wiped a tear from his eye. "Implications? It seems pretty specific to me. Apologists like you have been strewn all through history—you think the bible is literal up until the moment it's inconvenient, then you have to come up with excuses for it. Why don't you go ahead and read a little more? Entertain me. We have all night."

I put my Bible back in my pocket and crossed my arms over my chest. "I don't need to defend anything to you."

"No matter," said the demon. "I know all religious texts word for word—the Bible, the Vedas, the Talmud... all of them, but for your sake we'll stick to the Bible." He then began speaking in a language I didn't understand, but stopped abruptly after a few moments. "Oh, I'm sorry, would you like to hear that in English? The passages lose a lot of their impact when they're not in their original language, but I suppose there's no point if you don't understand it." He made a show of clearing his throat, then continued. "Everyone in Babylon will run about like a hunted gazelle, like sheep without a shepherd. They will try to find their own people and flee to their own land. Anyone who is captured will be cut down—run through with a sword. Their little children will be dashed to death before their eyes. Their homes will be sacked, and their wives will be raped." He stopped and looked directly at me. "Now isn't that just hilarious? Do you see why it's among my favorites?"

"You're only cherry-picking the passages that you think prove your point."

"Well, you must admit I've been given a lot of cherries to pick from. How about this ripe little one right here? Ephesians 6:5—Slaves, obey your earthly masters with respect and fear, and with sincerity of heart, just as you would obey Christ." The demon tapped his toes on the ground, seemingly giving me time to absorb what he said. "So Is that why you're here?" he asked. "Because you're the Pastor's good little slave? Subjecting yourself to my presence while he refuses to come and see me again?"

"I'm done responding to you."

"I don't want any more responses from you tonight," the demon replied. "Just listen to me as I recite more of your precious Bible to you."

I swallowed hard and stared straight ahead.

***

On my third night, I checked in at the rectory again. "You made it back," Pastor Johansson said, pleased. "I'll be honest, you've made it further than many of the others who tried."

"I almost didn't come in, but I wanted to prove I could do it."

"It's okay to prove it to yourself, but you don't need to prove anything to that creature. I hope that's not what you're feeling."

I glanced at my watch. "It's almost time for me to start."

***

I did the change-over with Eldon. He was far more tired-looking than the two previous nights. I greeted him kindly and took my seat as the door closed. The demon was in the corner of the room, sprawled motionless on the floor. I noticed almost immediately that it was wearing the same clothing Eldon had been wearing when he left. I stepped closer so I could get a good look at its face. Its eyes were closed, but even then I could see that it had taken the form of Eldon.

A chill descended upon me as the thought that maybe this really was Eldon on the ground before me, and the demon was the one who had just left the room. If that was the case, the pastor would have to be notified immediately. "Eldon!" I said. "Is that you?" It appeared that he was barely breathing. I reached my hand toward his shoulder, but I stopped just an inch or so away. I'd been specifically instructed never to physically touch the demon. Doing so would grant it the power to touch me in return—but this was Eldon, and he needed help, right? I blew some air on his cheek. "Eldon, wake up!" I shouted. There was no response. I reached in one more time, despite the voice in the back of my mind that was screaming at me to stop. I yanked my hand back when it was only a hair's width away from him. Instead, I stood up and slowly retreated back to my chair. A few minutes later, it seemed that Eldon had stopped breathing altogether. "Eldon, if that's really you, please forgive me."

Five hours—that's how long I sat in the room with a motionless Eldon. I can't tell you how many times I almost got up to try and check on him, but if that wasn't Eldon, then there was too much at stake for me to try anything at all. Then, the body lying on the ground spoke. "If you'd been paying more attention during your training, this little trick wouldn't have stressed you out so much."

I let out a sigh. The demon was still in the room with me. It sat up with a laugh. I was beginning to hate hearing that thing laugh.

"Do you like my Eldon impression?"

I simply folded my arms across my chest and looked at the wall.

"That's okay. You don't need to speak to me tonight. I've put you through enough already," it said. "For now, just listen, because I have a story to tell you. You like stories, right?"

I continued to stare at the wall.

The demon sat up and cleared its throat. "One day, about fifty years ago, there were three young men who lived in this very same town we're in now. They each loved the same young woman, and each of them was determined to be the one to marry her. They abandoned everything in their lives that mattered to them in order to woo her—their jobs, their friends. One of them had just gotten married and had a small child at home, but that didn't make a difference. He left them."

The demon glanced over to see if I was listening, and despite my attempts to appear uninterested, the look I had on my face seemed to please it. It continued the story with delight. "The girl, she was beautiful. And I don't mean that she was simply pretty. No, she was the most gorgeous thing ever created by nature. Her beauty was beyond anything that could be described by mere words, but you could say it was the kind of beauty that emperors would go to war over. And yet, here she was in this small, insignificant speck of a town."

My arms remained crossed, but admittedly, I was listening.

The demon kept speaking. "Now the three young men, they weren't willing to share her. Each one wanted her for themselves and themselves only. This led to many arguments and fights, so they decided that they would meet up in the woods, away from the hustle and bustle of the town, and have a serious discussion about which one of them was most deserving of the girl. This was an awful plan, because each of them had secretly brought a knife along, and it wasn't long before they began attacking one another. In the end, they all bled to death from their horrible wounds, while the girl watched from behind a tree and laughed. In fact, the girl had visited each of them separately the night before, and she was the one who had given them the knives as gifts."

"Why are you telling me this story?" I asked.

"Because it's hilarious. They stabbed and stabbed and stabbed one another. You don't see the humor in that?"

I shook my head.

"Well, to be honest, the story actually does have a tragic part to it, because one of the young men who died was a decamonoprogeny, which is a protected person the girl should not have involved in a deadly scheme. She'd failed to realize his true nature beforehand. It was one of the very few mistakes she'd made in all her existence. She became vulnerable and exposed—temporarily stripped of any power she might've had. In the end, certain people in the town began to understand what her true nature was, and she wound up getting captured and held hostage in a small room by a bunch of country bumpkins. Tragic, no?"

I looked at the demon, still in the form of Eldon. It actually had a sad look on its face. "Of course," the demon continued, "you're wondering what exactly a decamonoprogeny is. It's not a term someone like you would've heard." The demon stood up and started pacing. "It's an only child, of an only child, of an only child, and so on… it has to go back at least ten generations. They're rarer than you might think—almost impossibly rare, and like any rare creature, they're prized, and their lives are given certain protections. They're also incredibly difficult to detect." The demon stood up and stared straight at me. "Yes, difficult, but not impossible. The vast majority of them don't even know what they are."

"I don't care," I asserted.

The Eldon-demon, paying no attention to what I'd just said, instantly perked up. "But the story has a happy ending, because a few years later, as her power slowly returned, the girl was able to leave the room after she learned how to be in two places at once. The funny part is that the country bumpkins didn't even realize it." The demon gave a hearty chuckle. "In fact, the girl even went to visit your house earlier tonight. She talked to your mother and admired all the red roses that you have in front of the house. Oh, the yellow pansies are lovely as well. Your mother seemed quite proud of the way they visually pop out against the blue paint of the house."

My jaw dropped. The demon had just described my home.

***

"Mom, did anyone come by here last night?"

My mom put a plate of eggs and toast down in front of me. "It's kind of strange that you should ask, but yes. Remember that one pretty girl that you were in youth group with a few years ago? Susan, I think? After you left, she stopped by here."

My fork dropped from my hand. "Susan? I haven't seen her in a few years. What was she doing here?"

"I'm not too sure. It was right before sunset and I saw her outside admiring my flowers, so I went out to say hello. She told me she was out for a jog. Just getting some exercise, apparently."

"Did she tell you anything else?"

"Not much, really. She was sweet as always, I guess. Very complimentary of my roses."

I pushed my plate aside and stood up from the table. "Thanks, mom, but I'm not hungry. I think I'm just going to try and get some sleep."

***

I checked in with Pastor Johansson that night. "It told me that it escaped—that it can be in two places at once," I said.

"It's said that before. It's lying. It always lies."

"But it said it'd been to my house, and when I asked my mom if anyone had come by, she said that an old friend of mine, someone I haven't seen in years, had dropped by out of the blue."

"It will use trickery on you. It can probe your mind, and even probe the minds of those who are closest to you. It simply used a coincidental happening to its advantage."

"I just don't know how much longer I can do this."

"You have to keep your faith. We need you. You're doing the lord's work. As long as you ignore it, nothing bad can happen."

***

I walked down to the basement and did the switch-over, this time with a grey-haired woman named Sheila. She nodded kindly at me as we switched places in the doorway. "It's nice to see a new face around here."

"Thank you," I said as I stepped inside.

The door closed with a thud as I turned and looked at the demon. I paused for a moment when I saw that it had taken the form of my father, who'd died several years earlier. "I'm so happy you came back," he said.

I sat down in my chair.

He stepped up close to me, almost getting into my face. "So tell me, what did you do after your mother told you that Susan stopped by? Did you go up to your bedroom and think about her? Did you tell your mom about how you were secretly in love with Susan but never had the courage to tell her? Did you jerk off to your fond memories of her?"

I folded my arms and stared straight ahead.

"And when you were done jerking off, did you have to punish yourself by cutting another mark into your arm?"

My right hand instinctively reached over to my left arm, where the scars of hundreds of cuts were hidden by my long sleeve.

The demon continued, "Exactly how many cuts do you have in that arm of yours? Four... five hundred? I highly advise you to stop cutting yourself every time you jerk off. Enjoyment should not equal suffering, son."

"I'm not your son."

"And of course I'm not really your father, but seeing he was the one who put the crazy idea in your head that self-pleasure is a punishable offense, then maybe it would be best that he be the one to tell you that it's actually not. Perhaps many of the beliefs you cling to should be discarded, don't you think?"

I could feel my left arm tingling, as if all the cuts I'd made over the years were tiny worms squirming around under my skin. I scratched my arm reflexively.

"Bennet, do you remember that time when your youth group volunteered at the community center, and when you were done, all of you went swimming at the community pool? Susan was there too, right?"

Yes, I remembered, but I shook my head no.

"Remember what she wore to go swimming? It was a little more revealing than you expected, wasn't it? How many cuts did you have to make on your arm from that one?"

My arm continued to tingle, but I stewed in stone-faced silence while the demon went on and on, reminding me of all the times I'd lusted after Susan, who I'd loved from the first moment I met. I endured the verbal fusillade the entire night until Sheila came back to relieve me in the morning.

***

"Mom, do you think Dad was ever wrong about anything?"

My mom slipped a plate of pancakes in front of me. She seemed a little surprised by the question. "What brings this on?" she asked.

"I don't know. I was just thinking about him, I guess."

"Well, your father was human, like the rest of us." She paused to think through her next words carefully. "We didn't always agree on how to raise you, if that's what you're wondering. He was hard on you, maybe a little too hard at times."

"So that means you think he was wrong about certain things?"

"He always did what he thought was best. He never knew his own dad, and I think that always drove him to overcompensate a little bit with you."

I bit into my pancakes while I thought about everything that had transpired.

***

I went in for my fifth night in a row. Afterward, I would have a few nights off, which I was looking forward to. I did the switch-over once again with Sheila. I sat down in the chair and saw, to my dismay, that the demon had taken the form of Susan, the girl (and now woman) whom I'd lusted over for so many years. "Hey Bennet," she said casually. "How are you doing? It's been a while, hasn't it?"

It'd been five years, three months and ten days since I'd seen Susan, but I didn't take the bait.

"I missed you," she continued. "Remember all the fun times we had?"

She stepped closer to me. She was as beautiful as I remembered, perhaps even more so. Even the miserable florescent lighting couldn't dim the features of her exquisite face. But of course, this wasn't really Susan, right?

"Yeah, I know what you're thinking—that I'm not really Susan. But the truth is that it's been me the whole time."

"You're NOT Susan," I said defiantly.

"Well, I go by many names, but Susan is indeed one of them." She saw that I still wasn't fully convinced. "Just think back to when we all used to hang out together. Where did I live? Did you ever see my parents? Doesn't it seem strange that I was just always there, without having come from anywhere?"

I remembered back to the time when Susan and I had been friends, and though it had never occurred to me at the time, Susan's existence did seem a bit mysterious upon examination. The more I thought about it, the more I realized that, one day, she'd basically popped out of nowhere—no family that I remember, no real origin. Just sort of there.

"But why would you hang out with a bunch of church kids?" I asked.

"Because it was fun," she said. "Do you remember poor old Harold?"

Harold Rainer—he'd jumped off a bridge and killed himself.

She waited a moment for the name to sink in, then spoke again. "He wanted to fuck me, just like all the boys did. And when he couldn't, he decided he'd rather die. Oh, and do you remember Kevin?"

Kevin Brighton—he'd been hit by a locomotive. At the time, nobody was really sure if it was an accident or suicide, but it was now becoming plainly obvious that it was the latter.

Susan laughed as the memories of the dead boys flashed through my mind. "The truth is, I do my best work in the church," she said. "There are just so many desperate and conflicted souls. In fact, there are only three people who I know of in this congregation who are truly virtuous. Do you want to guess who they are?"

I knew, but I didn't say it out loud—they were the only three people who were able to maintain a vigil over the demon for any real length of time.

"That's right, it's those three," she said, apparently reading my mind. "And they've wasted their pious little lives under the mistaken belief that they were making any sort of difference at all. Even the Pastor didn't last long in here. Do you know he actually showed me his dick? I laughed at how small it was and then he cried. He wanted to fuck me but I wouldn't give him the chance. Just a simple touch from him would've unbound me from this room entirely, but I still rejected him because he's pathetic. He doesn't come in here anymore." She moved in close to my face, just a few inches away. I could smell a sweet perfume on her. "But your dick isn't small. You've got a big gun in those pants, don't you?"

Her sudden change in tone took me by surprise. But... the surprise was pleasant. She was wearing a loose top, and as she leaned closer, I was able to look down and see her bare breasts. I thought about turning away from the sight before me, but it was too marvelous and mesmerizing. I felt a stirring in my pants, which I tried to cover with my hand.

She shooed my hand away from my pants, nearly touching me, but still managing to avoid any real physical contact. "It's okay," she cooed. "Just let it happen."

I shook my head and finally managed to look away. "No! It's not right! Yesterday you appeared as my father, before that you were Eldon. You were a monster and a tiny little creature too."

"Those were just facades. I had to disarm you. I had to break you down so that I could rebuild you." She removed her shirt and her pants and stood before me completely naked. "Look at me. This is the true me, the form in which I was created. I am beauty. I am light." She leaned in so that I could smell the nape of her neck. I inhaled her scent deeply and felt myself growing bigger. "Go ahead and feel my breasts," she said. "I know you want to. It's okay."

No. It wasn't okay. Yet nonetheless a deluge of memories spun through my mind, making me relive all the times that Susan had smiled at me, or innocently brushed up against me, or casually leaned in to share a secret. There were so many times when I just wanted to hold her. But always, alongside those thoughts, was the voice of my dad, berating me, and telling me that my feelings were the embodiment of sin. I didn't want to listen to my dad any longer. I forced him from my mind—*Go to Hell, Dad. You've given me only emptiness. For once I choose pleasure.* His voice left me, and the squirming sensation of the scars on my arms ceased forever. He was truly dead, but Susan was right in front of me, alive and gorgeous. It was an intoxicating moment that ensnared my mind. As if I was on autopilot, I reached out for her breast and felt its perfection fill my hand. A pleasant warmth shot through my arm as I made contact.

"That feels nice, Bennet. You have such a gentle touch." She put her arm around me and sat down on my lap. "Keep going, there's no reason for you to stop now." She leaned in and kissed me deeply as my hands began roaming over her entire body.

***

I was spent. Susan and I were lying on the floor after hours of carnal pleasure. She'd let me do anything to her that I wanted, and I had taken full advantage of the situation.

Susan traced her finger along my chest. "Wasn't that wonderful?" she asked.

I nodded in agreement, but as I did so, my head began to clear from the enchanted fog that had taken hold of my mind. "Are you really Susan?" I asked her.

"You have to figure that out for yourself, lover. But just know that in the five nights you've been here, I only told you one teeny tiny lie, but it was the exact lie you needed to hear."

"What was the lie?" I asked.

She kissed my nose. "I'll never tell," she said with a devilish smile. "And that's the truth."

I thought back to what she said on the first night, about the best liars telling the truth most of the time. It seemed she was right about that.

She kept cooing in my ear. "And now, sweetheart, I need you to go home and castrate yourself."

"What!?"

"You heard me, my love. There's really no other way for this to end. Go home and cut your balls off, then wait for me. I'll come retrieve you when I'm ready."

My hands shot downward as I reflexively covered myself, yet at the same time there was a strange, nagging little part of me that just wanted to make her happy, or maybe I knew that my actions deserved punishment. Still, I protested. "I don't know if I can."

"Sure you can, sweetie. You're my prize and you'll do as I say. I have plans for you, so listen up. There's a nice sharp knife in your nightstand. You know, the one that you use to punish yourself." She ran a finger along the cuts in my arm. "It'll be the quickest way."

"It will hurt," I protested, desperately trying to think of a way to avoid the inevitable.

"Love hurts, baby," she whispered with her hot sinful breath in my ear.

"I don't love you."

"Don't lie to me," she said. "You've always loved me."

There was no room left for debate, and even though there was still a part of me that was screaming NO, I got up from the floor and walked to the door. I didn't even bother to put my clothes back on. I turned and took one last look at Susan—beautiful, gorgeous, naked Susan—and then opened the door and walked up the steps. I left the building and stepped out into the predawn air without a second thought.

I walked home at a brisk, determined pace, arriving while it was still dark. The knife was in my nightstand drawer, exactly where Susan knew it would be. As I picked it up, I could hear the sound of far-off emergency sirens. A momentary curiosity diverted me from my task. I stepped up to the window and brushed aside my curtains to see what was going on. On the horizon, there was an orange glow emanating from the church's steeple—fire.

I shrugged and let the curtains fall back into place. Back to the task at hand. Any last resistance I might've harbored had slowly dissipated. In fact, I'd come to a place of complete understanding. She NEEDED me, but she couldn't have me trying to fuck her all day long. Nothing would be accomplished like that. It all made sense—I would be far more useful to her this way. I lowered the knife down to my groin with a smile on my face, knowing that it wouldn't be too much longer before Susan came to retrieve me.

THE WELL, THE WHEEL, AND WILHELM

Karl Wilhelm's left arm was the first limb that was smashed. The executioner's club shattered it with enough force so that witnesses in the back of the crowd could hear the cracking sound clearly. He cried out in agony as he lay across the span of an old wagon wheel. His limbs were tied fast to the wheel's edge, and its spokes supported his body. The wheel itself was atop an old, unused well, and Karl stared heavenward as the executioner, encouraged and energized by the whooping and cheering of the crowd, dragged the large club along the ground as he positioned himself at Karl's right side. With all of his strength, the masked executioner brought the heavy instrument up above his head, and as the club reached its peak the crowd paused in anxious anticipation. The club fell down, cracking Karl's right arm under the blow. The crowd responded with uproarious cheer.

The man in the mask moved along to each of Karl's legs, breaking them both above and below the knee. Bone protruded through the torn skin as blood dripped through the ruptures and into the well below. The crowd screamed their approval and threw rotten fruit at the condemned man. The executioner removed his mask and raised his arms to encourage the crowd to cheer further. His last strike landed on Karl's chest, breaking several of his ribs. Blood erupted from his mouth and nose. With that, the executioner dropped the club and stepped away from the well.

From the back of the crowd, a boy of about ten studied Karl's gasping form. "He's still alive," the boy said to his uncle.

"That's all part of the punishment, Victor," his uncle responded. "He'll lay there in pain. Death will take him when it's ready. I've never seen a man who lasted past sunset." The boy continued to study the dying man through the other onlookers, many of whom were taking turns spitting and urinating on Karl.

Victor recalled the list of charges that Karl Wilhelm had been accused of. "What is lycanthropy?" he asked of his uncle.

"It means he can become a wolf. It's the mark of a wicked man."

Victor nodded his understanding. "Can we stay and watch him die?"

"I have work to do, but you can stay until sunset. Don't forget I need your help tonight at the tavern."

"I'll be there," Victor assured him.

As his uncle walked away, Victor could hear the broken man plead to the crowd with strained breaths, "Please, just kill me." This only encouraged the horde more, and they jeered and roared at his predicament. However, as the afternoon heat began to take its toll the excitement of the crowd began to wane. One by one, the men and women left for their cottages and hovels until only Victor and a few others remained.

The boy stepped closer to the dying man with uncertainty apparent in each step. When he was as close as he dared, he pursed his lips and launched a phlegm projectile that struck Karl between his eyes.

With great effort, Karl turned his head to where Victor stood. The two made eye contact. "So... thirsty," Karl rasped.

Victor stared at the face of the accused man. Each of Karl's brown eyes reflected the swirling white clouds above him. Longer and longer Victor stared, losing track of time and relinquishing awareness of his surroundings. He had no idea how long he maintained eye contact with Karl Wilhelm, but when he finally broke his stare, it was almost sunset, and the village square was nearly empty. Victor backed away from the wheel and its man, and as he headed off to his uncle's tavern, he felt a twinge of regret that he had spit on someone so defenseless.

His uncle's prediction, that Karl would be dead by sunset, proved to be entirely wrong. Those who lived nearest to the old well had their slumbers disturbed throughout the night as Karl screamed and moaned. His pleas for mercy and death went unanswered as the village residents held pillows and blankets over their heads in an attempt to drown out the horrid sounds of the dying man.

All through the next day, Karl continued with ungodly shrieks and screeches as death refused to take him. Residents who, just a day earlier, had made merriment at the man's suffering, soon found themselves anxious and disconcerted as his cries carried on throughout the day and into the next.

"Go get the executioner," some of them demanded. "Have him finish his job."

Others argued against that. "No, he'll die when he's supposed to. No mercy for the wicked."

On the third night after his supposed execution, Karl Wilhelm still appeared to be very much alive, as proven by his unceasing cries of pain and requests for mercy. From his uncle's tavern, Victor could hear him clearly between pauses in the conversations. Frazzled patrons lined the bar and occupied all the tables as Victor weaved in and out, bringing mugs to the tap for refilling and then returning them to the customers. Various discussions about the man outside dominated the night, and fear punctuated the dialogue as the men nervously proclaimed to understand what was going on.

"Hell doesn't want him, that's why he won't die!" proclaimed Peter the shoemaker. Others raised their mugs in nervous agreement.

"I don't think he's guilty at all," came a response from across the room. The men all paused and looked at Conrad Becker, one of the village's oldest men. "We're being punished—forced to listen to the cries of an innocent man until we ourselves go insane."

"How could he possibly be innocent?" others demanded.

"I looked him in the eyes, and I know the stare of innocence." The tavern became hushed as Conrad Becker spoke. "And why should we believe the allegations against him? Did anyone observe him turn into a wolf?" The men all looked at each other, waiting to see who among them would stand up as a witness. "The judges on the counsel are only interested in making a name for themselves. The truth doesn't concern them."

Victor's uncle spoke up. "Then who tore apart Walter Earnst? And who ripped his daughter's head off? A giant wolf was seen walking on two legs outside of Karl's farm, and his hatred of Walter was well known. That's close enough for me. Who else could it have been?" Cheers of agreement supported him.

Conrad protested. "That's not real evidence! Lots of people didn't like Walter Earnst! Some of them are in this bar right now!"

"Then who is the lycanthrope if it's not Karl Wilhelm?" the men asked as they began to break into smaller discussions amongst themselves.

They argued late into the night. Most seemed to agree that Karl Wilhelm was indeed guilty, but a few maintained his innocence. As the crowd dwindled, Victor said goodnight to his uncle and headed home. His trip was interrupted by the moaning of Karl Wilhelm. Victor's paces stopped, and after a moment's hesitation, he turned and walked toward the well, the wheel, and Wilhelm.

As he approached, Wilhelm's ears twitched and he seemed to sense Victor's presence. "Water," came his strained request.

Victor hesitated.

"So thirsty," Karl said in a raspy voice that was barely above a whisper.

Victor viewed the pathetic form in front of him, and a stitch of sympathy took hold. He looked to the dewy ground and saw a small dirty puddle where the night's condensation had collected. Glancing behind him to make sure no one was looking, Victor made a cup with his hands and bent down to gather as much of the water as he could. He carefully stood up and moved his hands over Karl's mouth. As he loosened his fingers, the water flowed down and dribbled into Karl's delirious maw. He repeated the act of mercy two more times until the puddle gave no more water.

"Thank you." Victor noticed that Karl's voice was noticeably less raspy.

"You're welcome."

Karl stared up into the starry night and enjoyed the sensation of a wet throat. Eventually, he spoke again to Victor. "My father taught me to never let a debt go unpaid, but I have nothing I can give you except for advice." He paused for a moment to think. "Always remember that the world exists in shades of gray."

Victor contemplated what was told to him but failed to understand what the man was getting at. Without saying anything more, he backed away slowly and left for home. Soon, any relief that had been visited upon Karl was gone, and his screams and wails started up. In their homes, the residents spent another night trying their best not to hear it.

Karl held strong throughout the next day. His pleas were ignored but not unheard, and nearly everyone within earshot was noticeably on edge. His gangrenous legs, chapped skin, and sallow features made him appear as something other than human to those few who wandered over to look.

That night, many of the residents again gathered within the tavern, thankful that the activity of the crowded room was able to drown out the noise from the man on the wheel. Ironically, they spent most of their evening talking about the very man they were trying to get away from.

The arguments from the previous night were far from settled, and Victor listened as the inebriated men took up their positions once again.

"Only a wolf-man could survive out there this long!" some claimed.

Conrad Becker, the primary defender of Karl's innocence, shot back, "If he was a wolf he would have changed into one by now! Clearly he's just a man, and only a man."

Victor tuned them out. The beers he brought to the men kept them slaked and heated at the same time. Soon, the air in the room grew thick, so Victor was glad when his uncle allowed him to take a break. He stepped outside into the fresh air and took some deep breaths. The first thing he noticed is that the night was quiet. Curiously, he walked over to the village square to check on the condition of Karl Wilhelm. The man was still breathing.

"Victor? Victor is that you?" the condemned man asked as he approached. Victor hadn't realized that Karl even knew his name.

"Yes, it's me."

"Thirsty…"

Victor reached into his shirt pocket and pulled out a flask that he'd earlier filled with water. He opened it and held it over Karl's mouth, allowing the liquid to slowly dribble its way down.

"That tastes good," Karl said. The two of them waited in silence as the man slowly regained some sense of humanity. "And now I must repay you." He stared at the heavens thoughtfully. "You will be better off in life to forgive past transgressions."

Victor considered the advice and then took his leave before anyone saw him talking to the living dead man. Karl's screams began again shortly thereafter.

Day broke, and the residents tried their best to carry on with their normal activities, but they found themselves becoming more and more irritable as Karl's moans pierced their ears and penetrated their minds. A small group of men, led by Conrad Becker, gathered in the village square. A few of them believed in Karl's innocence, while the others had simply had enough of his loud suffering and were anxious to see it end.

"That man should be put out of his misery," Conrad declared with an axe in his hand. The men nodded and hummed their agreement. With raucous cheers they headed to the wheel.

Victor, who was preparing his uncle's tavern for the night, heard the unfolding scene and went outside just in time to see Conrad lift the axe above his head, poised to strike down on Karl's skull. Even from across the way, Victor could see Karl's muscles relax, relieved that a finishing stroke was only moments away. Before Conrad could bring the axe down, the thunder of fast approaching footsteps was heard.

"Don't you dare end that man's life!" came a scream from behind Victor. It was Hans Stein, a prominent village leader who had sat on the counsel that had found Karl guilty of lycanthropy. He was accompanied by several other men.

"Can't you see what's in front of you?" Conrad protested as the second group made their way toward the well. He hesitantly lowered his axe. "Look! This is no longer a man, but a miserable wretch! Have you no mercy?"

Hans arrived at the well. "I agree that this is no man, but a wretch he is not. He's a wolf, and God or the Devil will take him when they're ready."

Conrad gave a once-over to the tortured man in front of him. Flies buzzed above the rotten flesh on Karl's legs. Deep cracks spread out over his skin like spider webs, revealing dried musculature underneath. His eyes appeared to have sunken deep into his skull, and his limbs were contorted at odd angles.

With resolve, Conrad lifted the axe back up with a shout. "Death is his only choice now, and the quicker the better!"

Before he could land a strike, two burly men came up from behind Hans and grabbed onto him, slamming him to the ground. The head of the axe fell onto Conrad's leg causing a long gash to form along his shin.

For a tense moment, it appeared as if the two groups of men were going to come to blows, but the determination of Conrad's group wavered as they all took turns waiting for someone else to act first. In the end they only stared at each other ashamed.

Hans took advantage of the lack of leadership within the rival group and spoke loudly, "There will be no intervening! All of you leave before you're arrested." He directed the two burly men to drag a semi-conscious Conrad away from the well.

"Please…" came the scraping voice of the man on the wheel.

Hans ignored the pleas and waited while the group dispersed. When he was sure the mob had disbanded, he too left, and Karl was alone in his agony. His pained moaning began yet again as the sun beat down on him.

Victor had watched the scene unfold with conflicted feelings, but soon he retreated back into his uncle's tavern where they were preparing for the nightly crowd.

"Uncle, do you really think that man is guilty of being a wolf?"

"I believe in the counsel," his uncle replied. "They say he is guilty, therefore he is guilty… and good for business," he added with a chuckle. He looked closer at Victor. "You don't think he is innocent, do you? You just take those concerns and bury them if you do."

"Yes, uncle," came the reserved reply.

Karl Wilhelm was indeed good for business, and that night the tavern was as full as it had ever been. It was only in the late hours that Victor had a chance to slip away. He stepped out of the tavern and into the cool air. Across the square, he could see Karl lying across the well. A low hum was emanating from his lungs, but it ceased as Victor approached.

"Victor? Is that you?" Karl asked with a wheezy whisper. His eyes, which were pointed directly up into the sky, were completely dried out and lifeless.

Without saying a word, Victor removed a flask and attempted to pour some water into Karl's mouth.

Karl shook him off. "Save it. I'm beyond thirst now."

Victor lowered his arms dejectedly, and both the man and boy remained silent in the cool night air. Victor could hear the crickets chirping for the first time in days. It was almost entrancing.

"Victor, do you know where my house is?" Karl asked to the surprised boy.

Victor took pause at the odd question, but affirmed with a murmur that he knew where the house was.

The visit from the boy seemed to energize Karl, and he spoke clearly. "Good. I have one more favor to ask of you. In the corner of the bedroom there's a loose floorboard. If you lift it up, inside you will find a common belt, just like the one you're wearing to keep your pants up."

Victor glanced down at his leather belt.

"Please, will you retrieve it for me?" Karl asked with a cough.

Victor scratched his head. "What do you want with a belt? How can it help you?"

"It was made for me by my wife nearly twenty years ago, right before she died. It's one of the only things I still have that reminds me of her. I believe she'll find me and guide me into the afterlife if I wear it."

The boy looked at the pathetic man in front of him who wanted nothing more than to die, then glanced back at the tavern, where the libations were still flowing freely and he knew he was needed. "I can't leave right now."

The sounds of vigorous arguing filtered through the walls of the tavern and littered the night air. Karl allowed the sounds to envelop him before speaking. "I promise, those men inside won't be angry with you." Then Karl sweetened the deal. "There are some gold coins hidden alongside the belt. They can be yours."

Victor considered his options. He knew his uncle would be upset if he was gone too long, but the promise of the coins intrigued him. "I can get it for you later tonight," he offered.

"I've waited here long enough, Victor. My house is only minutes away if you run fast."

The moon shone down upon the two of them as Victor finally agreed to the request. He wasted no time as he bolted off. His feet carried him quickly to the outskirts of the village, and then beyond. Down the trail he ran as the trees and thickets grew denser around him. Soon he found Karl's farmhouse, which had been abandoned since his jailing. He pushed on the front door, which creaked as it slowly opened. The house was completely dark inside, which forced Victor to inch his way to a window and push aside the ratty curtains. Bits of moonlight streamed into the room—barely enough for him to see. He crept further in until he made it into the back room of the home.

The rickety floor bent under his weight as he shuffled to the only unfurnished corner in the room. He knelt down to feel for a loose floorboard while the smell of dust kicked his nose. He methodically felt each board until a loose one moved in his fingers. He eagerly moved it out of his way and jammed his hand down into the murky hole. His fingers felt the belt immediately. He pulled it out and put his hand back inside, looking for the gold coins which he'd been promised, but he felt nothing more within the hole. Disappointed, he reached further in, feeling along the dirty crevices. There was only emptiness.

Victor knelt in the darkness mulling over his situation. Had Karl lied to him about the gold, he wondered, or had someone already come along and taken it? Either way, he knew his uncle was going to be furious, and he had nothing to show for his absence. He grabbed the belt, inched his way out of the gloomy dwelling, and pushed through the woods on his way back to the town.

He arrived back at the village square out of breath and exhausted. On his run back, he'd made the decision to bypass Karl and return directly to the tavern, but as he approached, the renewed moaning from atop the well gave him pause. He still had sympathy for the tortured man.

The moaning stopped as Victor approached. "Do you have the belt?" Karl asked.

"There was no gold!" the boy sputtered.

"I'm sorry. I lied to you about the gold," Karl replied between obvious bouts of suffering. "I had no choice."

Disillusionment crept along Victor's face.

"Please forgive me, Victor. I ask one last thing of you—put the belt around my waist."

Victor, who only wanted to go back to the tavern, decided to give the man his one last request and then be done with him for good. He climbed on top of the well and reached his hand under the man's back, threading the belt under and then over him. He closed the buckle and then jumped down from the well and started walking back toward the tavern.

"Victor!" came the suddenly much stronger voice of Karl Wilhelm, "Have you thought much about the advice I gave you?"

The boy stopped in surprise at how much stronger the man sounded. He ran through his previous conversations with Karl… shades of gray, forgiving past transgressions—he wasn't sure what it all meant.

"You see, Victor, I was a good man, but I still wanted to see Walter Earnst dead. He attacked my wife many years ago and never paid for his crimes… he was too close to the village counsel."

Victor returned to the well and noticed that Karl's eyes were no longer sunken into his skull. In fact, his entire face looked much healthier.

"So I called to the Devil, and it took years, but he answered. I wanted Walter Earnst to pay for his deeds in the most horrible way."

Karl's deflated muscles began regaining their form.

"It was he who gave me the belt, not my wife. Again, I'm sorry I had to lie to you."

Victor took a step back as he saw the broken bones in Karl's legs straighten out and heal.

Karl continued, "and when the deed was done, I was ashamed of myself because I had killed his daughter too. When they came to arrest me, I allowed it. I could've gotten away."

The wheel began cracking under the strain as Karl's growing limbs pushed against its rim.

Karl's voice grew deeper. "And I waited here for days, hoping for a death that refused to come. It finally became apparent to me that God won't have me, and the Devil thinks I still have more work to do."

In the moonlight, it appeared to Victor that Karl's very face seemed to be contorting into something different.

"So I'll do HIS work."

Coarse gray hair began growing upon his body as Victor sat frozen in fear.

Karl's voice had attained a deep, animalistic growl. "You've done me one last favor and, as before, I can only repay you with advice." He turned his head and stared at the boy. His eyes were yellow. "Run."

Victor fell backwards onto his bottom and crawled away. When he heard the wooden wheel begin to break apart, he finally stood up and heeded the advice, running away beyond the boundary of the village.

The wagon wheel splintered into pieces as the man attached to it doubled in size. His body contorted into a wolfen shape as he stepped down from the well and howled. Walking on two feet, the beast approached the tavern, while inside a sudden confused silence fell over the men. For the most part, they were the same ones who had laughed at Karl, the same ones who had spit and pissed on him, the same ones who had allowed his suffering to go on unabated. Karl owed them for five days of torture and agony, and as he entered the tavern through its only door, the single thought on his primitive mind was that he should never let a debt go unpaid.

GHOST FALCONRY!

ghost falconry
[gōst ˈfalkənrē]
NOUN

The sport of hunting with ghosts in the same manner as one might hunt with falcons; the keeping and training of such specters by a handler who is predisposed to seeing ghosts and the glowing auras generated by all living souls.

***

When it comes to ghost falconry, the best advice I can give you is to make sure the ghost you're paired with is very, very stupid. Smart ghosts are far too independent-minded and won't willingly bend to your wants and needs, so it's pointless to try and train them. All they'll do is ignore your instructions and go on nightly rampages of terror across the city, which yield you no profit. Even ghosts of average intelligence are difficult to mold and shape. Yes, stupid ghosts are the way to go—it might even be said that a stupid ghost is worth its weight in gold, if only it had any weight at all.

These below-average ghosts, by the way, are not so easy to find, but the effort is definitely worth it in the end. Chapter One of the Official Ghost Falconry Manual suggests that you peruse news articles to find someone who died a stupid and completely avoidable death, and then go to the place of their demise and attempt to capture the resultant spirit. My latest catch, for example, is someone who drowned in a toilet bowl. He wasn't even drunk, high, or suicidal at the time—just a below-average guy who somehow landed his head in a toilet bowl and couldn't manage to get his nose or mouth above the waterline before losing consciousness. Yes, there are probably some extenuating circumstances I'm not aware of, but when you learn about a death like this, you gotta jump on it before another ghost falconer beats you to it.

This leads me to my second point—not all people who die become ghosts. Most, in fact, do not. I can't tell you how many times I tried to track down the ghost of someone who died a stupid death only to find out that no ghost existed at all. It's a gamble, really, but as with any gamble, sometimes you get lucky.

So my toilet ghost, who I named Melvin, is basically my best find ever. He's just cognizant enough to respond to the training, but displays no desires of his own, except for his desire to feed. Wait a minute, you say. Ghosts eat? Well, yes, they do—they feed on bits and pieces of souls. Strictly speaking they don't HAVE to eat. I mean, they're already dead, but they certainly enjoy eating once they get a taste for it, and it helps to quickly restore their power after they've been active. For the most part it's harmless to the person whose soul is being harvested, unless it's a particularly ravenous ghost doing the harvesting. Melvin, like most trained ghosts, is careful to retrieve only the very edges of souls, and then bring them to me. Most people who've been harvested by Melvin retain more than ninety-nine percent of their soul and feel no ill effect. At worst, a few of them might feel momentarily irritated, but will quickly recover. So rest assured, I'm not really hurting anyone.

Melvin gets to eat half of what he harvests, which keeps him fat and happy. I get to keep the other half, which I can sell for cold, hard cash to a mysterious man who goes by the name of Phalangium. I have no idea what Phalangium wants with these bits and pieces of souls, but he always happily buys whatever I bring him. I've almost saved up enough to buy a used Honda Civic. The one I have my eye on has only a hundred thousand miles on the odometer and some sweet flame decals along the sides.

I keep Melvin in a fancy cardboard box that I painted purple (his favorite color). It also has some Latin incantations written on all six sides that help keep him under my control. The whole thing fits in my backpack, which allows me to walk nonchalantly through town until I find a mark (someone with a delicious-looking soul) that will keep both Melvin and Phalangium happy.

Last Saturday I was downtown doing a little hunting with Melvin. It was evening, so the crowds weren't too dense, which is actually the best time to hunt. After an hour I saw a great opportunity—a man and a woman eating at an outdoor dining area. The woman had a delicious-looking orange aura, while the man's aura was a beautiful swirling rainbow kaleidoscope (which is highly prized according to chapter two of the manual). As long as they both remained relatively still, Melvin would be able to take nicks out of both of their souls, and they would never even know it.

I sat on a bench across the street from my two marks. Slowly, I removed Melvin's box from my backpack and opened the lid. Melvin, who appeared to me as a faintly glowing orb with visible facial features and wispy tendrils for arms, poked his head out of the box.

"Psst," I said to get his attention.

His ears perked up.

"Those two across the street." I nodded in their direction. "Go get 'em, tiger!"

Melvin levitated out of his box and floated across the street, aiming directly for the couple. A few moments later, the woman swatted at the air in front of her, like maybe there was a fly there. Melvin dug his tendrils deep into her cranium.

"You okay?" the man asked.

The woman paused for a second and then nodded as she went back to eating her meal. One down, one to go. A second later, the man coughed as Melvin moved across the table and perched, imperceptibly, upon his shoulder. As with the woman, Melvin's tendrils dug into his cranium and nicked a bit of soul. Then, as soon as it had started, it was over. Melvin returned to my outstretched arm with his little hands full of glowing goodness that only he and I could see.

"Good boy," I said. Using my soul-splitting knife, I cut both specimens in half and held out Melvin's share in my palm, ready for him to consume. Once he was done, I took the rest and placed it in my soul-pouch. Two beautiful soul fragments—this would fetch me about fifty dollars. That Civic was nearly mine. I motioned to Melvin and he returned to his purple box, which I then stowed in my pack.

Suddenly, an explosion rocked the street, launching several parked cars into the air. The poor couple who Melvin had just feasted on were almost crushed as one of the cars landed right next to them. They got up and got the Hell out of there. People ran screaming down the street, away from the unfolding destruction, while at the same time a new man appeared from around the corner. I immediately noticed his solid blue aura, which, as explained in Chapter Three of the manual, could only mean that he too was a ghost falconer. He did a double-take when he noticed my own blue aura. "Thank the heavens!" he shouted. "A fellow falconer to assist me in battle!" I looked around, hoping he was referring to someone else, but he was for sure talking to me. "Yes, you! Fellow falconer! The war is not yet won. We must unite our forces if we are to defeat the spider demons."

"War?" I asked.

The new falconer looked a little confused, as if my question was the most insane thing he'd ever heard. "Yes, the war of the ghost falconers against the spider demons, with the fate of humanity resting in the balance. Surely you know of what I speak."

"Ohhhh that war." I looked down at Melvin, who popped out of his box and gave a little shrug.

"My name is Mordecai. I've tracked down one of the spider demons to this city. It's a particularly nasty one who seems to have developed a newfangled source of energy—almost like it's feeding off the citizens of the city themselves."

I stood eagerly at attention. "Wow, that sounds horrible. How can I help?"

"I've become separated from my team. Therefore I'll join up with you and we shall combine powers. With our strength, we can defeat this demon!"

This was a whole new level for me. A war was going on? That was news to me, but of course I was eager to help out my new companion. "How do we defeat it?" I asked.

"We'll use plan A17, as detailed in the Official Ghost Falconers Manual."

I had no idea what plan A17 was. "Uh, what chapter of the manual was that in?"

My new friend shot a look of surprise at me. "It's in chapter fifty-seven of course."

Okay, that explained a few things. Like any good ghost falconer, I had the manual at home, but at seventy-thousand pages long, it made a better doorstop than anything else. Heck, it could probably even double as an end-table. Admittedly, I'd stopped reading it after the third chapter. "Oh, right… that's the plan where we… where we…"

"Where we use our ghosts to throw cars at it," Mordecai said.

"That's the plan? Throwing cars at the demon?"

"Do you have a better idea? The manual says that in situations like this, landing a car squarely on the demon's head is the best way to kill it. But my ghost can't do it alone. He's exhausted, and his accuracy is compromised. Your ghost must help!"

A whole new world was opening up to me. Just a few minutes earlier I'd believed that the only purpose of ghost falconry was to suck out bits of peoples' souls so that I could buy a used car. But now there's a war? AND our ghosts throw freakin' cars? What else was I missing out on? I made a mental note to flip through a few more chapters of that manual once I got home.

"Okay, let's do it!" I said, my excitement growing. "Where's this spider demon at?"

The new falconer pointed down the street. "I've been chasing it for the last few minutes. It seems to be hiding behind that building."

I looked to where he was pointing and saw the demon's head poke out and look toward us. "Yep, got it," I said.

"Okay," he said, "it's time to unleash plan A17!" He pulled a golden, jewel encrusted box out from his backpack and opened it. "Behold the magnificent ghost Sullivan!" he said as his splendid glowing ghost floated upward. He pointed to a red

Toyota Corolla. "That's the car we'll use." He made a hand motion to Sullivan, who floated toward the Corolla and began lifting it. Mordecai looked back at me. "Now would be a good time for your ghost to help."

"Oh, of course." I pulled out Melvin's cardboard box. "Here's Melvin!" I said as grandly as I could. Melvin floated out of his box and looked at me. "Uh, Melvin, we're going to do plan A17." Melvin just stared at me. "You know, plan A17, where you help that other ghost lift the car and throw it at that spider demon down the street."

Melvin scratched his head. "Go ahead," I urged. "Help Sullivan throw that car." Melvin started floating away in the opposite direction. "No! the other way you stupid ghost!"

Something seemed to click for Melvin, and he turned around and flew toward the car. "Good boy," I said. "Now help him lift it up." Melvin made a lifting motion with his hands, essentially asking if he understood correctly. "Yes. Help him lift it up and throw it at that demon." Melvin nodded and began helping Sullivan. The two ghosts, working as a pair, managed to lift the car a good twenty feet off the ground, though it was clear Sullivan was doing most of the work.

The car started its eerie flight down the street when something began to go horribly wrong. Melvin was clearly struggling with his side of the car, which began wobbling back and forth. Sullivan tried his best to maintain control, but soon the car was spinning around in the air as the two ghosts tried unsuccessfully to coordinate their movements.

Mordecai ran toward them, shouting commands. "Steady, steady, don't let it go. Work together." It was no use. Melvin, completely out of his league, was far more of a hindrance than anything else. "No no, the other direction," Mordecai screamed. But he was too late. The out-of-control car did a full turn and came back the other way. It slipped from Melvin's hands, and a second later, Sullivan lost his grip as well. The Corolla dropped straight down and landed squarely on Mordecai. There was a grisly squishing sound as he instantly became the shape of a giant pancake.

Melvin looked stunned, while Sullivan began bawling hysterically. I motioned Melvin back into his box. "Let's get the heck out of here!" I said as I speed-walked both of us away.

"Who needs a war anyway?" The sound of approaching sirens only encouraged me to walk faster.

I hurriedly made my way over to Phalangium's residence, which is a cave hidden deep in the woods. When I got there, Phalangium seemed a bit out of breath, but he was totally happy to see me. "I see you have more of your product for me," he said in his deep, creepy-ass voice. As usual, it was too dark inside of his house to see anything, but I think he was smiling at the thought of more nourishment.

"Yes, look." I held up my catches for him. "I have some orange soul and some rainbow soul."

"I'm sure they're beautiful," he said. "As extra incentive for you, I'll be doubling my payout from here on out. It is more important now than ever that I receive your product."

"Great! Thanks man!" I collected my payment, ninety-seven dollars and twenty-three cents, and made my way out of the woods and to my house.

***

When it comes to ghost falconry, the next best advice I can give you is to not get involved in any silly wars. But was it true what Mordecai said? Was there really an ongoing war that I had kinda, sorta participated in? Right after I got home, I started flipping through my manual from the point where I'd left off a few years earlier. Chapter four was titled All Ghost Falconers Are at War with the Spider Demons. I buried my face in the palm of my hand. If only I'd bothered to read just one more page before giving up on the manual, I might've had second thoughts about taking up this pursuit.

Anyway, chapter four wasn't what I was interested in at that moment. Instead, I flipped to chapter fifty-seven—the same one that supposedly contained the spectacularly disastrous plan A17. When I finally found it, I saw it was titled *How to Use Your Ghost to Throw a Toyota at Spider Demons*. Score one for Mordecai, he apparently knew the manual backwards and forwards. I perused the pages:

Plan A1—How to Throw a City Bus at a Spider Demon

Plan A2—How to Uproot a Large Tree and Throw it at a Spider Demon

Plan A3—How to Uproot a Utility Pole and Swing it Like a Giant Baseball Bat and Hit a Spider Demon on its Stupid Head

…and so on and so on. It seemed pretty much any large object could be used as a weapon against these spider demons. I started to read more, but the dullness of the book quickly tired me out and I ended up falling asleep on the couch.

The next morning, my snooze was interrupted by the sound of shattering glass as three people came jumping in through various windows of my house. In the dining room, a noble-looking man came smashing in dramatically. "Behold!" he said, as if he was some sort of magnificent creature. "I am Johan, the Archduke of Ghost Falconry. And here is my ghost Winslet!" He pulled out a shiny box, perhaps the shiniest thing I've ever seen, and opened the lid. A majestic, pulsating green ghost arose from within. It was certainly beautiful.

The second person who'd smashed his way into my house took a similar approach to his introduction. "I'm Brutus Hull!" He pulled out a diamond encrusted box and proudly introduced his ghost. "And here is the mighty Lawgiver!" He opened the box, and a deep-purple ghost floated out—I have to admit, it was an unfathomably beautiful phantom.

The third person seemed to be a little more reluctant than the others as she cracked her way through one of my living room windows, but she finally made her way in. She surveyed the mess that she and her companions had created and seemed to feel a bit guilty. "Hey Brutus and Johan, maybe we should've just knocked on the door."

"Chapter sixty-four!" Brutus shot back.

"Yes, yes, of course," the woman responded. "We should always introduce ourselves as dramatically as possible." She reluctantly pulled out a simple wooden box. "I'm Pricilla, and here's Gracie!" she said as she popped open the lid. A puff of smoke creeped slowly from the box, but I failed to notice any sort of ghost. Pricilla's aura seemed a little off as well.

Brutus paid no further mind to Pricilla and looked straight at me. "We've been led here by the ghost named Sullivan. He seems to believe you know something regarding the disappearance of his handler, a team member of ours known as Mordecai."

"Oh yeah, that," I said. It seemed as though Sullivan had followed me. I scratched the side of my head, debating whether I should tell them the truth. "Uh, I think one of those spider demons squashed him with a car or something like that. He's no longer alive."

"Oh no!" Brutus and Johan shouted, almost in unison. They both grabbed their chests as if the news had given them heart attacks.

Behind them, I saw Sullivan float into my house through one of the broken windows, pointing an angry spectral finger at me. He flew right up to me and let his ghostly little tendrils linger over my face. "Stop doing that," I muttered under my breath. "It wasn't my fault."

Brutus, by then, had regained his composure. "We never should've let him come to this city alone, but he was just so eager to catch that spider demon that he didn't want to wait for the rest of us."

"Okay, well, there's three of you," I said, "so I guess you won't be needing my help any longer. If you could just pay me for my windows you can be on your way."

"On the contrary! You're a fellow falconer and must join with us!" Brutus said, conveniently ignoring the topic of my broken windows. "As the demise of Mordecai has shown, our kind does best when sticking together. And this is your city, you're certainly more familiar with its intricacies than we are."

"Yes. Please come with us," Pricilla said with a flat affect. "We'll get that spider demon for sure… if you help us."

I have to admit that Pricilla was kind of cute, and seemed far more normal than her two companions. Maybe spending some time with her wouldn't be such a bad thing. I blushed and nodded yes.

"Then it's decided!" Brutus proclaimed. "We'll hunt the spider demon as a team of four! Now please introduce yourself."

I picked up Melvin's box. "My name is Wick," I said, "and this is Melvin." I opened the box and waited for Melvin to arise.

After a few seconds of absolutely nothing happening, I shook the box vigorously. "C'mon Melvin. Show yourself!"

A few moments later Melvin poked his head over the rim of the box. But Brutus, despite having asked for an introduction, had already lost interest and was on his way out my front door. "Time to move!" he announced.

I picked up Melvin's box and followed them outside. "How do we find this spider demon?" I asked.

Brutus held his arm out, allowing Sullivan to float over to him and perch on his wrist. "Sullivan is an excellent tracker and has already encountered this spider demon once before. He will lead us!" He turned his attention to the ghost. "Sullivan," he said, "please lead us in the direction of the nearest spider demon."

Sullivan appeared tired. Instead of actually going anywhere, he lazily circled our group before landing on Pricilla's head. "Hmmm," Brutus pondered. "He most likely needs nutrition before he can be of any assistance. He must've been flying around all night." He turned toward me. "Tell me, where is the best place in this city to find people with strong auras?"

I stroked my chin, deep in thought. "Well, downtown is usually pretty good…" I trailed off after remembering the previous night's debacle starring Mordecai. "On second thought, let's head to the marketplace."

"Well then, let's go!" Brutus commanded. He turned to me. "We've been walking all night. We'll allow you to drive us."

I bemoaned the sweet Honda Civic which was not yet mine. "My car is uh… in the shop. But the marketplace isn't too far."

"Oh, I see. You should be commended for keeping your equipment in top condition, even if it means that for today, we have to walk." He gestured for me to lead the way, which I did.

We arrived at the marketplace a short time later, where several shoppers were lazily hanging around in front of the shops. One of them, a teenage boy, had a beautiful red aura with shades of green along the edges—we call that a Christmas aura. It was very unique, and as such, highly prized. It drew our attention immediately.

Brutus gestured with two fingers in order to draw Sullivan's attention to the boy. "Sullivan," he said. "You may eat."

Sullivan licked his ghostly little lips and flew over to the boy with the Christmas aura, latching on aggressively and sucking deeply into the poor boy's soul. Soon, the boy became pale and collapsed to the ground. Sullivan kept right on going, slurping up soul like he was finishing a milk shake.

"Hey, Sullivan is going to kill that kid!" I protested.

"Yeah," Pricilla agreed. "Call him off, Brutus. It's gone on long enough."

"Nonsense!" Brutus replied. "Sullivan needs sustenance if we're going to complete our mission. It's unfortunate that the boy must be sacrificed, but it can't be avoided. Blame the spider demons if it makes you feel better. They're the ones who cause us to take such desperate measures." Johan nodded in agreement.

"No way, man! There's got to be another way!" I screamed. A few people had begun to gather around the boy, while some others turned to look at us.

I pulled out Melvin's box and opened it. "Melvin, stop Sullivan from killing that kid!" It was a desperation move. Melvin and I had never practiced anything of the sort, but I was hoping that maybe my little ghost could rise to the task. Melvin surveyed the situation and surprisingly seemed to sense what needed to be done. He flew off in an instant and began zipping around Sullivan in tight circles, like an annoying gnat. Sullivan tried swatting at him but couldn't quite reach. Annoyed, he finally released his hold on the boy and began a full-on, rumble-tumble fight with Melvin. The two ghosts rolled up into a ball together and began throttling each other's necks. Luckily for Melvin, Sullivan hadn't yet had a chance to regain his full strength. The two of them were an even match.

They angrily entangled their tendrils to the point where it was hard to see where one ended and the other began. Eventually they began spinning around so fast that I couldn't even tell what was happening. It honestly reminded me of two cartoon characters fighting, where all you see is a cloud of dust with the occasional body part sticking out.

"Get 'em Melvin!" I yelled while making some encouraging punching motions.

"Yeah, get 'em!" Pricilla said.

"This is an outrage!" Brutus protested. "Let Sullivan finish his meal, and... what's happening to him?"

It became obvious at that point that Melvin had gained the upper hand, as he slowly yet surely began compressing Sullivan into a little ball. He kept the pressure on, and Sullivan got smaller and smaller and smaller, until finally, he disappeared entirely.

"What?! What happened?" Brutus stammered. "This is inconceivable! Where is Sullivan?"

Melvin, fatigued from his fight, fell like a feather to the ground. I ran over to him and scooped him inside his box without missing a step, then I kept right on running, trying to get as far away as possible from those other falconers. The less I had to do with them, the better. Behind me, Brutus continued his diatribe. "This is an outrage! This can't happen!" Then, he took things to a whole new level as he commanded his ghost from his box. "Rise Lawgiver. Seek revenge for Sullivan!"

Johan joined in, calling his own ghost forth. "Winslet! Arise and seek revenge for Sullivan!"

I ran hard until my lungs felt like they were going to burst. Despite my best efforts to get away, I felt a prickly sensation on the top of my head, and not a moment later, I felt my energy start to ebb. I stumbled and fell to the ground, while a purple haze filled my eyes. Lawgiver and Winslet had gotten hold of me. I tried to pick myself up, but my arms gave way and I fell flat on my face. Melvin's box hit the ground and skidded away. "Get away from me!" I screamed while helplessly swatting at the two ghosts.

As I started to fade out of consciousness, I felt a strong pair of arms wrap around my waist and lift me up. I wasn't too sure what was happening. All I knew was at that moment I seemed to be traveling very fast, almost like I was being carried by the wind itself. I felt the ghosts' hold on me loosen, and then give way altogether. I was free, then, I passed out.

I don't know how long I was unconscious, but I woke up in a park under the shade of a giant eucalyptus tree. Pricilla was looking at me with concern. "Are you okay?" she asked.

"I think so." I felt exhausted, like I'd just sprinted a hundred miles, but otherwise I was okay. "What happened?"

"We got away," she said.

"But how? Did you see how powerful their ghosts are? I should've been a goner... and wait! Where's Melvin?" I asked, realizing that his box was no longer in my hands.

"Here's his box," she said, holding it up. "I was able to pick it up with my free hand."

"It was you who saved us? But how?"

"Can I trust you?" she asked.

"You saved my life," I said. "You have my eternal trust."

She paused, searching for the right words. "Well... let's just say that spider demons can run very, very fast and are extremely strong."

"Okay, that's great, but what does that have to do with you saving me?"

Pricilla's eyes scrunched up with exasperation. "Really? You don't understand what I'm trying to tell you? I mean, I know ghost falconers aren't typically the brightest bulbs in the room, but..." She faded off, recomposed her thoughts, and then continued. "I'm a spider demon."

"But you don't look like a spider."

"Spider demons don't have to look like spiders, you know. We can be perfectly normal looking."

I took a moment to pay attention—really pay attention—to her aura. It had seemed a bit off to me before, but now that I took a close look, I could see pulsating blobs of gray permeating the edges of her otherwise dull yellow glow. "I've never seen an aura like yours before."

"Really? What does it look like?"

I'd been able to see auras almost my entire life, but this was the first time I'd ever been asked that question. "Golden," I answered generously, "with pulsating silver orbs along the edges. It's very pretty."

She smiled at that description.

"I have to be honest with you," I continued. "I didn't even know spider demons existed until yesterday. What exactly is a spider demon? I mean, what kind of thing are you?"

She seemed a bit insulted at the way I phrased my question. "Well what kind of THING are you?" she shot back. "Me? I'm a person—a woman born with rare and unique abilities that other people sometimes find scary and unnatural but shouldn't."

"Okay, but what were you doing hanging out with Johan and Brutus?"

"I'm a spy, sent to gather intel on what the ghost falconry community is doing."

"And those guys never figured out that you're a spider demon?"

She laughed. "Those two? They're total morons! Did you even see when I introduced myself to you? I don't even have a ghost in my box! I just rigged it to give off a puff of smoke every time I open it and they never figured it out. I can't even see ghosts! They're so focused on themselves and their so-called war that they didn't even realize there was a spider demon on their team. Ghost falconers are known for many things, but intelligence isn't one of them. It seems like your average ghost falconer trades thirty IQ points in exchange for the ability to see ghosts and auras." She noticed me frown, at which point she tried to backtrack. "Well I didn't mean you personally. You seem slightly smarter than most of the others I've met." She smiled.

"Okay, so I'm just a big idiot who can see ghosts. Why even bother to save me then?"

"Because you showed compassion for that boy. You and your ghost saved his life. You're clearly not an average falconer. There's something different about you."

I thought back to how quickly Johan and Brutus had shown their wicked side. I was nothing like those two. "Yeah, I guess I'm not an average falconer. But why didn't YOU try to save that boy? It seems like you could've done so pretty easily."

"I was about to intervene when you set your ghost loose. Maybe I shouldn't have waited, but I didn't really want to give up my cover unless I absolutely had to, which is what happened in the end anyway." She glanced around nervously. "We shouldn't stay here too long. Brutus and Johan might be multifaceted idiots, but in some ways they're savants, especially when it comes to hunting and tracking. They can be extremely dangerous if we're not careful. We're their number one target now and they won't stop until they get their revenge."

I grabbed Melvin's box and wobbled my way to a standing position.

"Can you walk?" she asked.

"I think I'm okay. Where should we go? I guess my house is off limits now."

"I have an uncle who doesn't live too far from here. He's more of a traditionalist than I am. He lives in a cave, actually. If we can make it there we should be safe. It's protected by ancient incantations that shield it from the falconers and their ghosts. Only people who already know about it, or are invited in, can see it."

"A cave in the woods? Sounds familiar," I said.

"You know of it?"

"I sell things to a guy who lives in a cave in the woods."

"What are you selling?" she demanded.

"Not much, just bits of souls that Melvin harvests from people around town. Nothing major."

Pricilla reached up and pulled out a clump of her own hair in apparent frustration. "Ugh! Just when I think I might have found the one decent ghost falconer it turns out you're stealing bits of soul and selling them… TO MY UNCLE?!"

"Oh, Phalangium is your uncle? Nice to know, but anyway I don't ever take enough soul to hurt anyone. I mean, what am I supposed to do with my ghost?"

"Uh, I dunno. Maybe NOT take things that don't belong to you. You don't have the right to take other people's souls. Not even little bits of them! Did you know that taking just a tiny bit of soul can have a long-term effect on someone? As a ghost falconer you should know this. It's in chapter twenty-three of your precious manual."

I suddenly felt ashamed. "Well, I didn't read that far. Nobody ever seemed too affected by it, so I just assumed it was harmless. And anyway, how do you know so much about the manual?"

"I had to study it before I could become a certified spy. And getting back to the subject at hand, I just saved your life, so to make it up to me, I want you to stop with your soul-harvesting."

She was determined, resolute and strong, and as her fierceness grew, so did her attractiveness. "Yeah, okay," I agreed. "You have my word. I'll stop." Goodbye Honda Civic.

"Okay, let's go," she said. "And I promise I'm going to have a real long discussion with Uncle Phalangium about what he's doing."

***

When it comes to Ghost Falconry, the next piece of advice I can give you is that you shouldn't listen to a damn thing I say. I tried to talk a big game. I tried to act like I was some sort of knowledgeable practitioner of an ancient art. The truth is that I don't know squat. Maybe I'm a bit guilty of being one of those (slightly) unreliable narrators—I dunno. But spending time with Pricilla has led me to reevaluate my priorities. So here's the whole truth. I've been able to see ghosts and auras pretty much my entire life—it's just a natural ability. The ghost falconry manual I have in my possession belonged to my grandfather. I have no idea why he had it, but I found it among his belongings after he passed away. I assume he must've been a practitioner himself, but he never said anything about it to me. Maybe he felt it would be better if I didn't get involved in some senseless war. After forcing myself to read the first three chapters, I went out and found Melvin, who really did die face-down in a toilet. He was my first and only ghost, and I'm lucky to have him. I'd been selling the soul fragments to Phalangium because I didn't know what else I could do with them. Until Mordecai came bursting onto the scene, I'd never met another falconer. For a long time, I'd lived in a fantasy world where I believed that ghost falconry was a noble pursuit, meant only for special people with special abilities.

We finally made our way to Phalangium's cave, both of us exhausted. Upon arrival, Pricilla gave a cursory knock on the door. "By the way," she said, "I think Phalangium is the same spider demon that Mordecai was chasing. It all makes sense now." I nodded my head in agreement as Pricilla gave one last knock and then simply pushed the door open. "Uncle Phalangium? Are you home?"

Pricilla paused for a moment and then moved inside, motioning me to do the same. A permeating gloominess greeted us as we entered. A moment later Phalangium's deep, creepy-ass voice echo throughout the cave. "Stop! Who is it!"

"Uncle, it's me, Pricilla. Turn on the light! Right this instant!"

There was a long pause, and then a click as the lights turned on. I was immediately impressed with the size and grandeur of the cave-home as the corners and deep recesses became fully illuminated. Phalangium, who I'd never seen outside of some shadowy glimpses, looked like a surprisingly normal person, if maybe just a bit worn down by life. "Pricilla! It's good to see you again," he said as he went to hug her.

Pricilla returned the hug with genuine affection, but as soon as the hug ended her disapproving nature reemerged once again. "So Wick here tells me you've been buying bits and pieces of soul from him."

Phalangium turned and looked at me. "Oh, yeah…" he said as his voice faded off. "Hey there. Nice to see you again," he said sheepishly.

Pricilla continued with her line of questioning. "Do you know how bad that stuff is for spider demons?"

Phalangium rolled his eyes. "Yes. I wasn't born yesterday. It's just that Wick has some pretty good stuff. It really helps me relax. You know… it takes the edge off."

"Wait a minute," I said. "It's like a drug for you? And I'm your dealer?" I almost couldn't believe it. I mean, I figured the guy had been using the soul as some sort of nourishment, but as I looked around and saw a bunch of rolling papers on the counter, I realized that he'd been rolling up and smoking all the awesome soul I'd collected for him, which doesn't make a ton of sense, but somehow the dude had been pulling it off.

Pricilla snapped me back to attention with her answer. "Yes! That's the situation exactly, and any self-respecting spider demon should know better than to mess with that stuff. Isn't that right, uncle?"

Phalangium looked ashamed. "It's just that I met Wick in a chat room, and he told me what he was collecting, and that he didn't know what else to do with it. And it was pretty obvious that he wasn't in cahoots with the ghost falconry community at-large, so I said to him, 'bring it over here and let me try it.'"

Pricilla wasn't giving up. "I looked up to you, Uncle. I still do. This is disappointing."

Phalangium sighed and sat down on the couch. "I'm not the same spider-demon you used to look up to. I'm tired, old, and sick of being hunted. I just wanted to experience something new and exciting."

Pricilla, seeing just how deflated her uncle was, adjusted her tone. "That's how that Ghost Falconry Patrol guy found you, you know. You were this weird anomaly that kept popping up on the radar. The ghost falconers could sense what you were doing, but they couldn't pinpoint your exact location."

"Until I left the protection of my home," Phalangium concluded.

"Exactly," Pricilla said.

"I went out to see a movie. I guess I stayed too long. And that's when that weird-talking ghost falconer found me and started chucking cars all over the place. Well I won't make that mistake again. I'm staying put from now on." He took a moment to study her face. "They're chasing you too, aren't they? Just look how exhausted you are. It's obvious you've been fleeing."

Pricilla looked at the ground as if she was ashamed. "Yeah, we might have to stay here for a little while, if you don't mind."

"Of course I don't mind. You can stay here forever if you want. There's plenty of room and plenty of food."

Pricilla took the invitation as an opportunity to finally relax. "Thanks, uncle," she said with a relieved sigh.

And that's how we became Phalangium's houseguests. The protection provided by the home's enchantments didn't extend too far beyond the boundaries of the cave, so none of us could venture too far. However, the home itself was supremely comfortable, with a ton of rooms, cozy leather furniture, colorful tapestries, and funky cool lamps situated throughout. Phalangium really should've been an interior decorator based on what I saw. And let's not forget about how awesome Pricilla is—she kept me highly entertained! She's funny, she has a great laugh, and (when she's not busy judging people) she's the most relaxed person I've ever known. She told me a bunch of cool stories about the historic battles that took place between ghost falconers and spider-demons, and I taught her all about auras, and what the colors meant. It's rare to find someone that you can just spend the whole day talking to and never get bored, but that's how it was with me and Pricilla. I dare say, the days I spent with her were immensely enjoyable.

As for Melvin, his recuperation was slow yet steady. I had nothing to feed him, so he was a bit lethargic for the first few days, but eventually he regained his energy. Once he was back to full strength, the three of us invented a game called Where's Melvin, where Melvin would zip around finding hiding places and Pricilla would try to guess where he was, based on the clues I gave her. It sounds stupid, I know, but it kept us entertained when there was nothing else to do, especially when Melvin would find a silly hiding place like a box of Cheerios or something like that. A lot of times Pricilla would guess correctly on her first try, and then I'd tell her she was wrong, just to keep her from getting too full of herself.

After about a week of hiding, Pricilla and I, both beginning to suffer from a bout of cabin fever, decided we would venture outside for a late-afternoon hike. A bit risky, yes, but the idea of staying cooped up any longer simply didn't appeal to us, and Pricilla figured that as long as we didn't stay out too long, Lawgiver and Winslet wouldn't have enough time to sense our location. We walked through the woods, just enjoying the chirping of the birds and the chattering of the squirrels. Finally, she asked me to point to the tallest tree I could see. When I did, she told me to hang onto her back, and then proceeded to climb the tree, barehanded, with me holding on. Her strength and agility are simply amazing.

When we got to the topmost branches, we sat down (carefully) and watched the sun set over the tops of the trees. The light illuminated her face in a way I hadn't seen before. "You have a pretty smile," I said.

She blushed.

"Really, you do," I insisted.

For the first time, Pricilla looked a little timid. "Do you want to see me in my spider form?"

"What's that?" I asked.

"All spider demons have two forms, their human form and their spider form. Nobody outside of my family has ever seen me in my spider form," she said. "You'd be my first, but I know I can trust you."

I hesitated, not knowing exactly what she would turn into, but I quickly realized that everything would be alright. "Okay, show me," I said.

Pricilla took a deep breath, and then, sitting on a branch a hundred feet off the ground, she slowly transformed into something that... looked a lot like her human form, just more fantastic. Her blue eyes blackened into shiny obsidian marbles. From her shoulders, two additional sets of arms stretched out into the air, reminding me somewhat of a Hindu goddess. Overall, her appearance was a little more muscular, but when she was done, she still looked like the Pricilla I knew, maybe even prettier.

"Wow," I said. Her aura, which had previously been dull, had become the brightest shade of lavender that I'd ever seen. Lavender auras usually signified strength and honesty (per Chapter 3, Subsection iv). There was a perfectly beautiful silence as I continued to take in her sight.

"You know," she said after a moment, "spider demons aren't really demons at all. It's just a name that someone came up with a long time ago. I hope you know by now that you have nothing to fear from me, or anyone like me."

"I already knew that. I just don't understand why Johan and Brutus would want to hurt you."

"The ghost falconers like to act as if they're fighting some noble war, but really they're just hunting us down one by one. After so many generations, I don't think anyone even knows the reason why anymore. It's just always been this way." She looked at the horizon in contemplation. "And I want to thank you," she added.

"For what?"

"For being the only person outside of my family to ever trust me, and for being the first person to be interested in who I really am. I've never actually had the chance to make a true friend."

"You're welcome," I said. "And I want to thank you for showing me that there's more to life than just stealing bits of souls so that I can afford a used car."

Pricilla snorted out a giggle. The sun was starting to set, bringing our perfect moment to a slow end. Pricilla transformed back to her human form. "Grab onto my back and I'll climb us down," she said.

After reaching the forest floor, we walked back to Phalangium's home, which was bathed in silence. "He's already passed out for the night," she said with a smile. "Do you want to come see my bedroom?" she asked shyly.

I pondered that question for a moment—I'd already seen the inside of her bedroom from the hallway, and it looked a lot like mine—maybe a few square feet bigger. I couldn't really think of a reason why I needed to see it, so I just shrugged.

Pricilla seemed to sense the various directions that the wheels and cogs in my head were turning. She stepped closer and gave me a quick kiss on my lips and then asked one more time. "Wick, do you want to see my bedroom?"

At that point I finally understood what she was asking. "Yes," I said as I straightened up in excitement. "I would very much like to see your bedroom. Every last inch." She took my hand and led me inside. We closed the door behind us and didn't come out until the morning.

***

When it comes to Ghost Falconry, the next bit of advice I can give you is that if a pair of ghost falconers are looking for you, eventually they will find you. It says as much in the manual. We couldn't stay at Phalangium's home forever. Even with its protective charms we knew that the two determined falconers and their ghosts would stumble upon us eventually, if only on accident. So we were faced with two choices, the first of which was to try and run away. This would entail leaving the area, possibly even the state, quickly enough that they wouldn't sense us. According to Pricilla, this was how a lot of spider-demons lived their lives, trying their best to evade detection and avoid entanglements. We also had the option to stand our ground and fight.

It was Pricilla who finally decided the course of action we would take. "I don't want to run away anymore," she explained. "I'm sick of it. And besides, this town is your home. If you leave here you'll never have another place where you feel safe.

Believe me, I know the feeling of not having a place where you feel safe, and it sucks."

"But if we defeat Brutus and Johan, will we really be safe? Won't there be other ghost falconers ready to take up the chase?"

Pricilla shook her head. "Well, I'll always have to be on the lookout, but if we can get Brutus and Johan off our trail, it'll give us a lot of breathing room. They're the ones who have our scent, so to speak."

So it was decided: we were going to stand up to them. But to do so, we would probably need more help. Melvin had regained his full strength, but he was a single ghost who had never been trained past chapter three of the manual. True, he'd gotten the better of Sullivan in their scuffle, but we couldn't count on that type of luck holding up. Pricilla, as strong as she was, had a major disadvantage in that she couldn't see the ghosts we would be fighting against. And Phalangium? He wanted nothing to do with any sort of faceoff. I guess his last trip away from home had spooked him badly. According to Pricilla, he'd been quite the fighter in his day, but he'd grown skittish and tired in his older years. He did his best to convince Pricilla to just stay at the cave house and continue to lay low, but her mind had already been made up.

I pondered the situation until I came up with a pretty good idea. "Maybe we should get a second ghost to help us out," I suggested. "I think I can control two of them at the same time, if I get some practice in."

Pricilla thought about it for a moment and then nodded. "You know, that might not be such a bad idea," she said. "To be honest, I don't really support the idea of capturing and training ghosts, but we're in a jam. Maybe we should try it."

I'll admit I felt a smidgeon of pride when Pricilla liked my idea. "Not so bad for a dumb ghost falconer, eh?"

"Don't call yourself that," she said as she grabbed my hand and held it gently. "You're so much better than they are. Just because you share their abilities doesn't mean you have to identify with them."

"Yeah, you're right. Old habit."

She gave me a kiss before refocusing. "Okay now. Where can you acquire another ghost?"

"Not just any ghost," I said. "A dumb ghost."

"What about Mordecai?" Pricilla asked. "The guy might have been a decent ghost falconer, but in pretty much every other way he was as dumb as a bag of rocks. And the way you described his death to me... I mean the guy didn't even have enough sense to get out of the way of a falling car."

"Hmmm... Mordecai?" My mind flipped back to the memory of him getting squashed by the falling Toyota. "That might just be crazy enough to work. We'd be sending him up against his former friends, but as long as he's dumb as you say, then it really shouldn't matter. But that's only IF he's a ghost."

"Well, let's go check it out and see if we can find him," Pricilla said. "I'm sick of sitting around here all day."

I nodded in agreement and the decision was made. Mordecai's ghost, if available, would be my next capture. Pricilla, Melvin, and I left Phalangium's home before dawn the next morning and hiked back into the city. It was risky. Every moment we spent away from the cave was another moment we could be discovered. We moved quickly and purposefully. Pricilla kept a keen lookout for Brutus and Johan, while I scanned the skies for signs of Lawgiver and Winslet. If they spotted us, we'd be hopelessly outmatched and would have to make a run for it.

After a long, careful trek, we made it safely to our destination right as the sun was rising. We were the only ones around. "That's the spot," I said.

"Okay," she replied with trepidation in her voice. "We're way out in the open. Pay close attention to our surroundings." Her eyes scanned the rooftops. This was the first time I'd seen her nervous.

I flipped open the lid to Melvin's box. "Melvin, I need you to patrol. Let me know if you see any other ghosts."

Melvin stayed in his box, scratching his head.

I shook his box. "C'mon little dude! I need you!"

Melvin peeked up over the rim of his box.

"It's okay Melvin, just keep a lookout." I made the hand motion for him to patrol, and he hesitantly floated out of his box and began flying large circles overhead. I started scanning the area for any signs of ghostly activity. I looked up and down, left and right, and in every nook and crevice, hoping to see the little sliver of light that would indicate the presence of a ghost. And then, on a small grassy area in front of an office building, I saw a faintly glowing blue orb lying on the ground, peeking out from underneath a pile of leaves. "Got 'em!" I said. I kneeled and called to the ghost like you might call to a dog. "C'mon boy," I said. No dice. Mordecai's scared ghost seemed to be quite at home hiding underneath that pile of leaves. It was then that I remembered that I hadn't even brought a box for him. He and Melvin would have to share. I stepped up to Mordecai's ghost, treading gently to make sure I didn't scare him away. Once I was within reaching distance, I used the box lid and scooped him inside.

Once the new ghost was secured, I called Melvin down, motioning him to get inside too. He looked into the box, then stared icy daggers back at me. "I'm sorry," I said. "I know you don't want to share, but it's the only way."

Suddenly, I heard Pricilla yell at me. "Watch out!" She darted toward me at inhuman speed and knocked me aside as an airborne car came flying right at me, missing by inches. "Hold onto me!" she ordered. Melvin overcame his reluctance and zipped into his crowded box while I climbed onto her back, doing my best to hang on. I turned my head and saw Lawgiver and Winslet giving chase, while their two masters screamed commands at them. The ghosts were quick, but Pricilla was even quicker and got us out of there right as another car came flying at us.

When we got back to Phalangium's home Pricilla collapsed in exhaustion. "Did we lose them?" she gasped as she sprawled out on the floor of the cave.

"Yeah, the ghosts kept up for a while, but… damn you're fast."

"Yeah, I'm fast, but fast isn't always good enough. If we had to go any further, I don't think we would've made it."

"We'll we DID make it, so let's check out this new ghost." I tilted Melvin's box and shook it until Mordecai's ghost came oozing out. "Hey there little guy," I said. "Look at you. We gotta get you a name." According to the manual, it's important to give your new ghost a name as soon as possible. It helps them shed their former identity and makes the training go so much easier. "Mort, maybe?" I picked up an old shoebox from a nearby shelf and dusted it off. "Here you go," I said as I scooped him inside.

"No, too close to his original name," Pricilla said.

Phalangium, who was walking to the kitchen, passed by and looked at the box. "So is that where you're keeping the dead bastard who tried to smash me with a car?" he asked.

"Well, yes," I said, "but he's been through a lot, so maybe you shouldn't scare him."

"Whatever," he said with an eye roll.

"Good day, uncle," Pricilla said sternly.

Phalangium knew better than to push his niece too far. "Good day," he said pleasantly as he grabbed a soda from the refrigerator and returned to his bedroom.

"I'm tired," Pricilla said to me as soon as we were alone again. "Let's get some rest, and tomorrow we'll begin training…" she thought for a moment, "Oceanus."

"That's what you want to name him? Oceanus?"

She nodded her head. "Yep."

"Okay then. Oceanus it is."

Early the next morning we began our training. Melvin was included too because, lord knows, he needed it. It was lucky for us that Pricilla, due to her study of the Ghost Falconry Manual, had a far better understanding of how to train a ghost than I did. We made a good team.

And now we've gotten to the point where I'm going to avoid boring all of you with the mundane details of how to train a ghost. Instead, just imagine the ghosts practicing a whole variety of drills, like lifting up boulders, flying around in really tight circles, and doing one-armed ghost pushups. Now imagine Pricilla shouting directions at the ghosts, and then me telling her that she's looking in the wrong direction. And last, imagine that you can hear the theme song to Rocky while you watch all of this, like it's a movie training montage, and then you'll have a good idea of what the week was like as the ghosts and I whipped ourselves into shape.

And then (drum roll), we were ready. Or at least as ready as we were going to be. We really couldn't risk hiding out any longer. We figured the best place to face off against Brutus and Johan would be the auto junkyard that was just a few blocks away from where we'd found Oceanus. It was an ideal choice for many reasons—it was empty, so no innocent people would get hurt, and the stacks of junked cars would give us plenty of opportunity to duck, weave, and hide. And Pricilla reckoned that with so many potential projectiles lying around, Brutus and Johan would become overconfident, making our mission just a tad bit easier.

We left Phalangium's house before dawn, nervous, excited and scared all at once. A little while later, we arrived at our chosen battle site without incident. I surveyed our surroundings and then opened the ghosts' boxes. "Begin patrol," I instructed them. "Go now!" Both ghosts confidently arose from their cardboard domiciles and floated about thirty feet overhead. They commenced flying in figure-eight patterns. They were good to go.

Pricilla was on high alert, but she took a moment to look at me. "Thanks for being here with me," she said. "Too often we spider demons just run and hide. It's like we don't even know how powerful we are. But I'm sick of hiding. I'm sick of seeing my friends and family get squashed by busses and trees and boulders and shopping malls."

Shopping malls? I shook off the question as I caught sight of a disturbance overhead. Melvin and Oceanus both began frantically pointing their glowing little tendrils toward the entrance to the junkyard. My eyes darted to where they were pointing, and I saw Johan and Brutus approaching.

"Well well!" Brutus said. "We've finally found you." He and Johan wasted no time in opening their boxes and releasing Lawgiver and Winslet. Brutus allowed Lawgiver to float into the sky and then turned to address Pricilla directly. "You who hid among us in a web of lies—you'll be crushed like a common spider." He then turned and looked at me. "And to the traitor, no mercy will be given!"

I gulped nervously as I imagined what Brutus and Johan could do to me. What if they unleashed plan A3 and used a utility pole against me like it was a giant baseball bat? That could really hurt, and the worst part is that I'm allergic to pine wood, so I'd probably break out in hives while I was lying there all squashed on the ground. I quickly forced that unhelpful thought from my head as I slinked behind a junked car. Pricilla stood out in the open, seemingly defenseless. Brutus and Johan made smooth hand gestures, cueing their ghosts to move toward a nearby station wagon. A moment later, with the creaking of old metal, the station wagon was lifted into the sky. The ghosts worked in tandem and, from a distance, they flung the vehicle directly at Pricilla, who easily ducked out of the way as it crashed harmlessly behind her.

Lawgiver and Winslet would have to get closer—throwing cars from a distance wouldn't work against Pricilla. And THAT was our plan, to draw the ghosts in, far enough away from their handlers so that Melvin and Oceanus could sneak around the backside and subdue Brutus and Johan. But for the plan to work, Pricilla had to keep putting herself out there as bait, making herself an easy and obvious target.

Brutus and Johan took the bait and commanded their ghosts to move closer to us. I have to admit, there was just a tiny part of me that was disappointed when they fell for our plan so easily, only because I wanted Pricilla to see that maybe ghost falconers aren't so dumb after all, but those two thick-skulled halfwits never considered that they might be maneuvering into a trap, which, now that I think of it, was probably a good thing.

I ducked behind a car, nodding to Pricilla to let her know that the ghosts were approaching. From that point on, her reflexes would have to be lightning quick. Motioning for Melvin and Oceanus to follow me, I snuck behind a row of junked cars and worked my way closer to our adversaries. Thankfully, the minimal brain power possessed by Brutus and Johan was focused squarely on Pricilla, which meant they more-or-less had forgotten about me.

As I advanced, I heard the creaking and groaning of another car being flung toward Pricilla. I popped my head up just in time to see her dive out of the way of a red sports car. Too close, I thought. As fast and strong as Pricilla was, she couldn't last forever out there. Another car flew toward her before she even had a chance to get back up. She rolled to her left as it smashed to the ground beside her. If I didn't hurry she would be squashed, and that would be awful. I'd never met anyone as beautiful as her, and even though I'd still love her if she was a pancake-shaped smudge on the ground, her normal shape was much more preferable.

Once I was close enough, I motioned for Melvin to go and suck out some of Johan's soul—not enough to kill him, but just enough to incapacitate him. I ordered Oceanus to do the same thing to Brutus. My ghosts behaved beautifully, with both of them setting upon their marks without being noticed. The plan was working perfectly, right up until the point where I heard Pricilla scream. I turned and saw two cars flying at her. She couldn't dodge them both, and while one sailed harmlessly to her right, the other one nailed her head on, sending her flying backwards at least fifty feet. Any regular person would've died instantly, but Pricilla was still alive. Seriously injured, but alive. Flat on her back, she woozily tried to sit up, but fell back to the ground in a heap.

At that same moment, Johan and Brutus began to show the effects of their souls draining, with their hands dropping lazily to their sides. *Keep going* I motioned to my two ghosts.

I turned back around to check on Pricilla, only to see a large delivery van floating toward her. It seemed as if Lawgiver and Winslet were carrying out the final order they had been given. They carefully positioned the van over Pricilla and then floated with it higher and higher, obviously planning to let it go once they reached a great height. She would be squashed like a spider under a shoe if I didn't do anything.

"Melvin! Oceanus!" I called. "Save her!" Melvin glanced up from the best meal he'd ever had. Even with his little ghostly pea-brain, his training kicked in and he immediately recognized the danger. He left his mark and zipped toward Pricilla as Lawgiver and Winslet ascended with the van in their tendrilly little grasps. Oceanus, perhaps because he was so new at being a ghost, ignored my calls and kept sucking out Brutus's soul— Melvin was on his own.

Lawgiver and Winslet must've gone over a hundred feet in the air before they released the van. "Don't let it land on her!" I screamed. Melvin flew faster than I'd ever seen him go, becoming a streak of white light as he shot through the junkyard. All of his new training really seemed to be paying off. He collided with the van just a moment before it landed, altering its trajectory just barely enough to avoid squashing Pricilla.

"Great job, Melvin!" I yelled as I ran over to check on Pricilla. When I got over to her, I saw she was bleeding from...

everywhere it seemed. "Pricilla!" I said as I kneeled next to her. "Are you okay?" She gave no response. My thoughts shifted back to that magical moment when we were atop the trees, and it dawned on me that I was watching yet another sunset, except this time instead of sunlight it was the beautiful light of Pricilla that was receding from the Earth. Her aura pulsed feebly as she struggled to take in breaths. I held her close, trying my best to imagine that we were back upon those heavenward branches.

I was brought back to the present when Lawgiver and Winslet zipped past me like a couple of angry gnats. Luckily for me, they'd expended a considerable amount of energy throwing cars. Melvin, on the other hand, hadn't expended himself nearly as much. I motioned to get his attention, then directed him toward the two ghosts. "Go send them to the beyond!" I said.

Melvin zipped toward his targets. The two other ghosts didn't even see him coming. He grabbed Lawgiver first, flattening him out and folding him up like a sheet. He made smaller and smaller squares until there was nothing left. Winslet tried to dart away once he saw what'd happened to Lawgiver, but he was too spent, and Melvin easily caught him and began compressing him into a smaller and smaller ball, until he too simply disappeared.

I pumped my fist in momentary elation at Melvin's decisive victory, but as my attention returned to Pricilla, any bit of elation was soon overwhelmed by my growing distress. She didn't look good at all—her breaths were becoming shorter and shorter, not to mention all the blood she'd lost. "Pricilla," I said between sobs. "You have to wake up. I need you. I didn't realize how pointless my life was until I met you."

Melvin floated down and perched on my shoulder as I helplessly clung to Pricilla's hand. He even attempted to wipe away a tear falling from my cheek, even though his tendril passed right through my face. "This is awful, Melvin. All she ever wanted was to feel safe, and I let her down. I wasn't fast enough."

Pricilla began violently convulsing as the final threads of life she clung to were cut, one-by-one. "Please NO!" I sobbed in desperation. Then, at the moment of my deepest pain, Melvin unwrapped himself from around my shoulder and positioned himself so that he was right on top of Pricilla. He spread his tendrils out across her body, and then something amazing happened—glowing pulses of energy began to run along Melvin's ghostly outline and entered Pricilla. As best I could tell, he was transferring his own remaining energy into her. Within a few moments, Pricilla's convulsions stopped, and as the energy continued to flow into her, her breathing stabilized and her eyes flickered open. Melvin, after expending the bulk of his life force, floated gently away, as if he'd been set adrift upon the surface of a slowly meandering river. "Are you okay?" I asked Pricilla.

"I think so," she said. "What happened?"

"It was Melvin. He saved you. Twice actually."

She managed to give a smile. "Thank him for me."

I looked over to Melvin, only to see him drifting listlessly, barely visible at all. I held out my arm to call him over, but he simply shook his head no. He had nothing left in the tank. He wanted to obey me, but he simply couldn't. I stood up and walked to him. "Melvin, you were amazing," I told him. "You've done things today that I didn't even know were possible. How did you learn all that stuff?"

Melvin gave a little smile and pointed to his head, letting me know just how intelligent he really was after all.

"Yes, you're very smart," I said. "A lot smarter than I gave you credit for. I've learned so much from you."

Melvin looked skyward and then waved goodbye, flickering out forever. "Goodbye Melvin," I said. "I'll miss you."

I looked back at Pricilla, who had managed to sit up. Her life had been returned, while Melvin's existence had been taken away in trade. I truly would miss him, but I somehow felt at peace with the situation, as if that's how things were meant to be all along. "Can you walk?" I asked her.

"I think so." It took Pricilla a few minutes to regain her strength, but soon enough she was able to hobble around with my assistance. When we got back to Oceanus, I discovered that he'd finished off both Johan and Brutus, sucking out the entirety of their souls and leaving them as nothing more than two emaciated, prune-like corpses.

"You went too far, Oceanus," I said as I motioned for him to return to me. He burped, wiped his face, and then flew back into his box as directed. With our hunters vanquished, we left the junkyard.

***

When it comes to Ghost Falconry, the final thing you need to know is… nothing. I'm done with it. I could no longer, in all good conscience, keep doing what I was doing. It had never been our plan to kill Johan and Brutus. We only wanted to incapacitate them so that they would surrender and leave us alone, which is a perfectly acceptable outcome according to the Ghost Falconry Manual. You could certainly make the argument that they got what they deserved, but I never wanted to be a killer. It's just not how I envisioned my ghost falconry experience would pan out. I'd lost control of Oceanus and two people died as a result. And it's not just that, I was beginning to see that capturing ghosts might not be in their best interest, even if they willingly performed. In the end, I think it was just Pricilla's positive influence on me that caused me to reevaluate everything. I wanted her to be proud of me. So no more ghost falconry. I would just have to find another way to make use of my special set of skills.

A couple of weeks after our showdown, I took Oceanus out to a pretty meadow where I commanded him to rise out of his box. "Okay, this is it," I said. "I release you to the great yonder." He seemed a bit confused, so I gave him the hand signal that let him know it was okay to cross over to… wherever it was he would go. He looked hesitantly at me, but then he smiled and flew high into the sky, disappearing forever in a shower of sparks. He was gone, and the final chapter in the book of Mordecai/Oceanus had been written.

As for Pricilla, she's pregnant and she doesn't even know it yet. It seems like our night together at Phalangium's yielded some unexpected results. I know this because I can see a pure white light emanating from her belly. It took me a while to fully understand what it was, but then I realized it must be a new aura that was separate from Pricilla's. I thought about telling her, but I think she'll enjoy discovering her pregnancy on her own, and besides, she's so much smarter than me that I kind of enjoy the feeling of knowing something that she doesn't.

I can only imagine how powerful this child is going to be, because I've never seen the aura of an unborn child before. For its aura to be strong enough to reach out beyond its mother is simply amazing. Just looking at it makes me feel calm and oh-so content. Pricilla caught me staring at her belly and wondered why I had such a goofy smile on my face. I just gave a happy little laugh and kissed her on the cheek.

I've already purchased a book called Fatherhood in One-Hundred Easy Steps, and this is one manual that I promise I'll read from beginning to end. I've got a big job ahead of me, and I know there will be some major challenges, but I plan to take this more seriously than I've taken anything else in my life.

Speaking of manuals, the Ghost Falconry Manual, chapter 178, says that a leader of sight and strength will come forth to end the war between the falconers and the spider demons. Maybe it'll be my kid? That would be nice. Regardless, I see this as a chance to bring something really good into the world, as I've seen a lot of bad things recently and I'd like to think that maybe, just maybe, something can be done to balance it all out.

A DELICIOUS REVENGE

The dog, with her inquisitive eyes and powerful nose, noticed the rock-monster unfurling itself along the hiking trail long before her human companion did. She gave an excited yelp to warn of the upcoming danger, but her human didn't seem to catch on, and insisted, with a pull of the leash, that they both keep moving forward. "C'mon girl," she said, "we still have a few more miles." The dog's reluctance acted more as a distraction than a warning, keeping the woman oblivious to the creature, which only moments earlier had appeared as a small boulder strewn among the landscape.

Slowly, the former rock seemed to be transforming into something that was not of this world. Had the hiker been paying attention, she might've likened it to an armadillo unrolling itself, yet this was something far more sinister. Emerging from a deep slumber, the rock-creature began to stand and stretch its limbs, at which point it was finally noticed by the woman. "Whoa!" she said in surprise as the dog's ears flattened to its head.

After a long skyward stretch of its arms, the rock-creature, having grown to the size of a child, quickly came to attention and snapped its fingers at the woman. "Your name. What is it?" it demanded.

"I'm Carla," she replied hesitantly, as her eyes darted back and forth to see if anything else was amiss.

The rocky creature sized her up. "You look good Carla. Good enough to eat, even." Carla took a pensive step back. "Oh, you'll be going nowhere, I'm afraid." The rocky armadillo creature snapped its fingers again, casting a spell onto its pitiful prey. "Now, you'll do everything I say. First, get rid of that miserable beast next to you. Tie it to a tree or something. I won't have it getting in our way."

Carla, mesmerized, tugged the reluctant and whimpering dog away from the clearing and tied her leash to a low-hanging branch of a pine tree.

"Perfect. Come sit down. It's time for our dinner date." The rocky armadillo creature sat down, legs crisscrossed, and pointed to the spot directly in front of it. Carla obediently sat down. "My name is Ordan, and I've lived in these woods for over two-hundred years."

Carla nodded in acknowledgment while studying Ordan's craggy face and slate-grey body.

Ordan glanced over to Carla's backpack. "What do you have in there? Any food?"

"Just some granola bars."

"Hmmm, those don't sound delicious at all. The last person I ate was carrying a bottle of… ketchup was it? It made him so much tastier. You don't have any of that, do you?"

Carla shook her head. "Just the bars."

The disappointment was visible across the lines and crags of Ordan's face. "Fine then, you'll be tasty either way. So anyway, what month is it?"

Carla opened her mouth to answer but was interrupted by the frantic yelping of her dog.

"Tell her to shut up!" Ordan demanded.

Carla turned to the dog. "Maxine! Be quiet!"

Maxine gave a couple of pathetic yelps and then began pacing silently back and forth as far as her leash would allow.

"Your dog is lucky that I don't eat such dirty animals. Now, where were we? Tell me, what's going on in the world? Have any new wars been started? Any major disasters happen lately?"

"Why are you asking me questions? I thought you were going to eat me," Carla droned.

Ordan snapped some fingers at Carla once again, strengthening the enchantment. "I lead this conversation, not you. As I already said, this is our dinner date. And on a dinner date there's talking, and there's eating. This is the talking portion. The eating will come later."

Carla contemplated the question for a moment. "Hmm, it seems like there's always a war somewhere in the world. And disasters happen all the time."

Ordan's gaze pierced through Carla. "Are you always so boring and non-committal? The last guy talked my ear off for an hour. This is your last day on Earth, so please learn to carry a conversation. I only get dates like this once a year, so don't make this a wasted opportunity."

"Wars are bad. Natural disasters are bad. Not something I really want to talk about," Carla droned.

Ordan gave a big sigh. "Maybe I should've just let you pass by, but I don't sense anyone else in the area, so I guess it's you or nobody." She drummed her fingers on the rock beside her. "Let's try this again," she continued. "You can ask me a question, and let's see if that jumpstarts our conversation."

Carla pondered for a moment. "What's going to happen to Maxine after you eat me?"

"Concerned for your dog?" Ordan gave a hearty chuckle. "Maybe a bear will get her, or maybe she'll just starve to death. Or maybe one of a million other things will befall her. It doesn't really matter and I don't particularly care."

Carla's eyes glistened with tears of sadness as their dinner date descended into an awkward silence. Ordan's growing disappointment showed with the tapping of fingers. "You're not supposed to be crying," Ordan said in exasperation. "You're a horrible conversationalist. Let's just move on to the appetizers. Give me your hand, please."

Carla obediently raised her hand and moved it toward Ordan, who grabbed it and yanked it close. "I love the fingers. Not much meat on them, but tastier than you might imagine. They're like little sausages with a nice bony crunch. Take the rings off, please."

Maxine watched from the other side of the clearing as Carla struggled to take off her rings. Suddenly, she noticed some movement back beyond the tree line. What could possibly be out there? Whatever it was, neither that new creature nor Carla seemed to take notice. She gave two quick, excited barks. *Carla, look over there!* Carla, however, remained focused on her rings, finally removing them from her fingers.

"Thank you," Ordan said, while shooting a nasty look toward the annoying dog. "Now give me back that hand." Carla obediently raised her hand again so that her date could inspect it like a piece of meat. "Looks good." Ordan began cautiously gnawing on the pinky finger. "That doesn't hurt, does it?"

"I feel nothing," Carla said as little trickles of blood started flowing from her finger and into Ordan's mouth.

"Okay good. My charms seem to be holding up well. It really spoils a meal when your food won't stop screaming." Ordan nibbled at the finger a bit longer but then stopped abruptly. "Are you sure you're not carrying any ketchup in that bag of yours?"

Carla opened her mouth to answer, but was cut short when Maxine began yapping wildly and pulling at the leash that bound her to the tree. It was at that point that Carla noticed, over Ordan's shoulder, four dark shapes emerging into the clearing from the woods.

Ordan, oblivious to the approaching creatures in the background, shook an angry finger at Maxine. "I do wish that dog of yours would be quiet!"

Maxine simply continued with her frantic yelping, causing an annoyed Ordan to give up on trying to chastise her and return to the meal at hand. The succulent raw pinky soon found its way back into Ordan's mouth, but before much more of the meat could be torn free, Ordan noticed the shift in Carla's gaze. "What are you looking at?" came the rude demand.

"There's a pack of wild dogs behind you," Carla said matter-of-factly. As if on cue, the lead dog, a sinewy German Shepherd, let loose a vicious growl.

Ordan's bloody smirk dropped about a mile. The other dogs in the pack joined their leader, creating a growling crescendo heard by the other forest animals wide and far. The rocky armadillo creature shot upward to a standing position and turned around to look at the commotion. The four dogs might've looked familiar, if only Ordan had bothered to pay any sort of attention to the pets who'd accompanied some past victims. Ordan immediately realized the seriousness of the situation and considered options on how to deal with the pack. The dogs, all of whom looked ready to attack, could be defeated, but it would be a fifty/fifty proposition. Perhaps, Ordan surmised, rolling back up into an impenetrable rock and waiting for the situation to pass would be best. It would mean giving up on the current meal, but there would always be others.

Without waiting another moment, Ordan fell to the ground and began to return to a boulder shape. The dogs lunged forward, intrinsically knowing that if they allowed the creature to return to a rock form, their opportunity for attack would disappear. The German Shepherd landed the first bite, clamping onto Ordan's hand only moments before it could retract completely. The three others followed suit, each one grabbing onto a limb and pulling on it, causing Ordan to scream in pain for the first time in two-hundred years.

The rock-creature found some inner strength and was able to kick off one of the dogs, who went flying across the clearing and landed on its back. Next, Ordan swung an arm wide, ripping it free from the grasp of the German shepherd. Maxine, still tied to the tree, barked desperately as the struggle unfolded in front of her. Carla sat unfazed at the unfolding melee, still in a daze from the rock-creature's charms.

Ordan proved to be more formidable than any of the dogs had anticipated. With wildly swinging limbs, the rock creature caused the last two dogs to release their grips on her. The German shepherd urged her pack onward with a wild bark as she moved in for another attack, landing a bite on Ordan's knee before getting thrown loose again.

Ordan stumbled a few steps away from the pack and again started curling inward, almost regaining rock form when two of the dogs managed another last second attack. Ordan responded with rapidly swinging arms, sending the dogs flying. The pack, now becoming exhausted and weary, paused their attack. Ordan smiled, knowing that these dogs simply weren't strong enough to complete what they'd started.

It was at that moment, the moment of their defeat, that the pack found a new inspiration. Maxine, who had torn loose from her branch, found her inner beast and charged toward Ordan with a mighty snarl. She managed to latch onto one of Ordan's arms and yank hard. The rocky armadillo creature let out a shrill yell that seemed to inspire the pack. One by one, the dogs renewed their attack, grabbing an arm or a leg and pulling outward, exposing Ordan's soft underbelly. The German shepherd, smelling blood, latched onto Ordan's unprotected throat.

Ordan tried to command Carla to help fight against the dogs, but the words only came out as gurgles as the blood flowed freely from the gaping hole being torn open by the German shepherd. Soon, the rock creature's guts spilled out entirely as the bloody dogs celebrated their kill with loud howls.

Over the next half-hour, each of the pack members took a turn feasting on the moist, delicious innards. It was the best meal they'd had in years, and they didn't stop until the only remainder of Ordan was the inedible rocky backside. Maxine, still tame, resisted the urge to feast and went to her human, who'd fallen to the ground unconscious.

Once the pack was fully sated, they began to retreat back into the woods, one by one. Before leaving for good, the German shepherd approached Maxine and sized her up. This new dog had proven her mettle and would make a fine addition to the pack. The German shepherd gave a high-pitched bark directed at Maxine. *Join us.*

Maxine took a step toward this fascinating, courageous dog, but stopped short when she heard Carla, who was still under the charm of the rock creature, gasping for breath. She turned around and nudged Carla with her snout, at which point the human's raspy breathing stabilized. Maxine circled once and then laid herself down next to Carla. It would be getting dark soon, and the human would have to be kept warm and protected until the charm wore off completely.

The German shepherd watched all of this and thought back fondly to the human that she herself had once hiked the woods with. How she missed him. She gave one final bark to Maxine. *I understand.* Then she turned and disappeared into the forest with the rest of her pack.

Printed in Great Britain
by Amazon